Zombie Democracy

NEIL A. COHEN

PERMUTED
PRESS

A PERMUTED PRESS BOOK

ISBN: 978-1-68261-688-8
ISBN (eBook): 978-1-68261-834-9

Cover art by Christian Bentulan

PERMUTED
PRESS

Permuted Press, LLC
New York ▪ Nashville
permutedpress.com

Published in the United States of America

CONTENTS

Introduction 5

Chapter 1:   MEAT the Press 7

Chapter 2:   Strange Bedfellows 21

Chapter 3:   A Bellwether State 23

Chapter 4:   Third Party 29

Chapter 5:   Zomblog: They Promised Us
              an Apocalypse 34

Chapter 6:   Smother..39

Chapter 7:   Focus Group 46

Chapter 8:   Chum 50

Chapter 9:   The Hunter, the Soldier,
              and the Shepherd.......................................57

Chapter 10:   Live from Trenton 68

Chapter 11:   Religion and Politics 72

Chapter 12:   Pray vs. Prey 79

Chapter 13:   Antidote for Mortality 86

Chapter 14:   The Camp: Part I..94

Chapter 15:   The Camp: Part II 99

Chapter 16:   WTF Are Acronyms 104

Chapter 17:   The Camp: Part III 111

Chapter 18:   The Camp: Part IV.................................... 115

Chapter 19:   Kitchen Table Politics............................. 120

Chapter 20:   Honeymoon Period 127

Chapter 21:   Foreign Contribution 137

Chapter 22:   Identity Politics 145

Chapter 23:   Ancient Régime.................................. 150

Chapter 24:   Growing the Base............................... 155

Chapter 25:   Crossing the Aisle.............................. 158

Chapter 26:   Lars and the Long Ride Home 165

Chapter 27:   The Absence of Light......................... 169

Chapter 28:   Citizens United 173

Chapter 29:   The Tick 176

Chapter 30:   Build that Wall 185

Chapter 31:   Cloture 187

Chapter 32:   Hardening 191

Chapter 33:   Plenipotentiaries 196

Chapter 34:   State of the Union 203

Chapter 35:   Post Convention Bounce.................... 206

Chapter 36:   COOP SOUP.. 211

Chapter 37:   Breathing New Life into the Campaign..... 214

Chapter 38:   Bridge-Gate....................................... 218

Chapter 39:   Peaceful Transition of Power.............. 220

Chapter 40:   Eat the Rich 227

Chapter 41:   Inflicting Policy 230

Chapter 42:   Disinformation 240

Chapter 43:   The Government They Deserve............ 244

About the Author... 247

INTRODUCTION

Writing a book that riffs on current day events is always tricky. The writing process involves a period of proof reading, editing, re-writes, second-guessing, blurb requests and cover design. Once the book is finalized and the content is locked down, it goes in queue and waits for its assigned release date, which can take months. The result is that by the time the book is released, topics that were burning up the internet at the time of writing are now as cold as last week's tweets.

I always intended the *Exit Zero* Zombie trilogy to serve dual purpose. I wanted the story to provide a unique and hopefully entertaining zombie tale. But I also considered it to be a political allegory. *Exit Zero* was written during President Obamas term in office. The sequel *Nuke Jersey* was written during his second term, and *Zombie Democracy* was written during the 2016 Presidential campaign and the first one hundred days of the Trump administration.

What constitutes as a true Zombie Democracy is in the eye of the beholder. Just as any politician or political party can be viewed differently, I view a zombie democracy as I would view a newly infected zombie. Something that on the surface appears familiar and manageable, yet in reality, it is something that is totally out of your control. Something that will react violently if threatened. A zombie democracy, like any zombie, will never relent in its pursuit to destroy you once you have entered its sights, and will not stop until there is nothing left of you to consume. The best you can hope for is that a different, more appetizing victim, stumbles into its path, allowing you the chance to escape, but only at another's expense.

No matter where you are in the world when you are reading this book, if you feel you are living in a Zombie Democracy, and you're your friends and family are telling you that you are either paranoid, a conspiracy nut, a right-wing whacko or a left-wing lunatic, don't be dismayed. It could always be worse. Just relax with the confidence that things can always get worse.

My fellow Americans, thank you for your vote of confidence in electing to buy this book as well as surviving *Exit Zero* and *Nuke Jersey*. I hope the trilogy will serve you well.

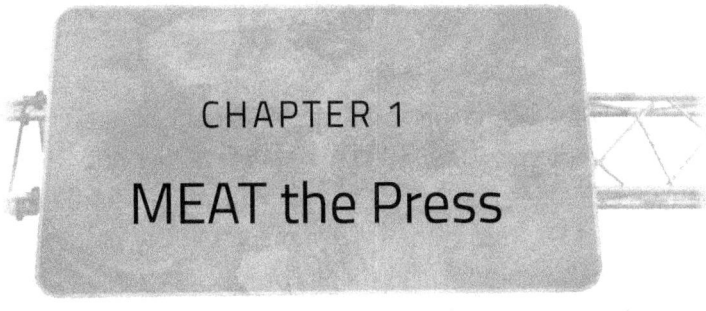

CHAPTER 1

MEAT the Press

"Hello, I am Olivia Barry and you are watching WRIX Channel 9 News at five.

"Our lead story, President Callahan's newly appointed Chief of Staff Harry Rose fielded questions today from an international press corps who have been ravenous for information. Due to ongoing security issues, a pool reporter was chosen by random lottery to solely pose the questions to Mr. Rose.

"We are proud to announce that New Jersey's own WRIX's Channel 9 News reporter, Clifford Scott was chosen as the representative for the domestic and international press."

The television screen displayed a live shot of reporter Clifford Scott standing in front of the Cape May, New Jersey hotel that had been serving as the White House since the Skell virus outbreak. The building is heavily fortified with concentric rings of stone and steel barricades topped with concertina wire.

"Clifford, the new Chief of Staff has had his hands full today. You really peppered him with questions. Tell us about it."

Clifford Scott, wearing a WRIX Channel 9 windbreaker, flashed his perfect news-hunk teeth.

"That is correct, Olivia," he said taking over the report. "It has been over a month since freshman Congressman Patrick

Callahan was sworn into office as President of the United States. He is the only surviving member after our prior President, the Cabinet, the Congress and the Senate, all tragically died on live TV. This is the first formal interview granted by the new Callahan administration. Not much is known about Chief of Staff Harry Rose, other than he previously led the new, and controversial, Security and Recovery Agency. Security and recover officers, known as Contractors, have become ubiquitous here in New Jersey and rumored to be deployed nationwide soon. The mission of the agency personnel is to provide security and stability for the public during this turbulent time."

"Clifford, these Contractors are the men and women wearing tactical uniforms that have been patrolling the state; enforcing curfews, and manning checkpoints?" Olivia interjected. "I know many of our viewers have expressed their concerns that these forces are paramilitary and don't display their names on their uniforms, just four-digit numbers. Did you bring those concerns up with Mr. Rose?'

"I did Olivia. The administrations rationale behind the numbers rather than names was that they needed to staff up so quickly that they did not have time to customize each uniform and thus, had only numbers embroidered for individual identification. I know that answer may not sit too well with everyone." Clifford replied.

"This virus and the effects it has on those that have become infected is terrifying. But security is not all this agency provides, is it Clifford?" she asked.

"That is correct." he replied.

"Once the agency is notified that infected individuals have been spotted, the Contractors are dispatched to carefully collect and quarantine them."

"Has the administration released any figures on the amount of people who have become infected and how many others have died since the initial outbreak?" Olivia asked.

Clifford shook his head. "The administration has not released any figures, but has assured us that the infection is under control and infected individuals, sometimes referred to as Skells, are being humanely quarantined. Despite these assurances, the security situation here and nationwide is still tenuous. International flights in and out of the United States, as well as interstate travel are heavily restricted. Many people in the country see the United States as a police state now. The current administration has pushed back on these claims saying that these security measures while extreme are for the safety of all citizens and are within constitutional law. These safety measures are also to make sure that containment of the virus is successful.

"I was given a limited time with Mr. Rose, so I hope my questions address our viewers most pressing concerns. Here's the interview."

The screen changed to, a single camera, two-person shot with a confident looking Harry Rose sitting across from Clifford rigidly in his chair.

Scott:"Mr. Rose, first off, congratulations on your position. We know very little about you. Can you give us insight on some of your background?"

Mr. Rose: "My background is really not that interesting, but I have served both this administration and this country since the initial outbreak, and I hope that I can provide continued support to bring us back to a state of normalcy."

Scott: "You use the term normalcy. Right now, we have an uncontained virus, of unknown origin continuing to spread across the country, infected individuals are going through what can only be described as a biological mutation, we have a PCRC security force which appears to be a combination of military and law enforcement patrolling the streets of the nation, we have infected individuals being picked up by PCRC Containment teams and being carted off to unknown quarantine areas, known as Q-Zones. Mr. Rose, is this the new normal?"

Mr. Rose: "That's a lot to unpack, but let me try. As you know, this is an unprecedented situation, a true pandemic. We did not feel that local law enforcement was equipped to handle the situation. We also did not want to turn the United States into a military occupation zone; so, we have not asserted Title 10 to deploy our armed services domestically. The National Guard is dealing with the Texas secession situation, but that is all. We have engaged the Post Conflict Restoration Corporation to hire, train and deploy their PCRC Security and Recovery teams, which will provide for the public's safety."

Scott: "Let's discuss the Post Conflict Restoration Corp, or PCRC. That firm was at the center of the horrific foaming scandal. The public was told the infected were being housed and cared for until a treatment could be found. As it turned out, the infected individuals were being ushered into PCRC *constructed warehouses, which were then filled with fire retardant foam that was suffocating the infected. How is PCRC still allowed to oversee the rounding up and housing the infected?"*

Mr. Rose: "The PCRC foaming scandal was a tragedy and no one was more disgusted and angry to learn about this atrocity than the President. This disgraceful activity was carried out by a rogue group within the company. As you know, PCRC founder and Chief Executive Officer Maxwell Gold is currently a fugitive and is being sought. Once found, he will stand trial for his crimes.

"As for the virus, we have all heard the claims by the cyberterror group known as Green Rights Action Schutzstaffel, or G.R.A.SS. They are spreading rumors the virus was created by PCRC. We have investigated this claim and have found no evidence to back that accusation. G.R.A.SS is a criminal organization that is focused on attacking both the United States government and our capitalist system. They have made outrageous claims about other corporations in the past. The true cause of this virus is being investigated and researched and I am sure we will soon find an inoculation and a cure."

Scott: "Will anyone else from PCRC be prosecuted for the foaming scandal?"

Mr. Rose: "As I said, the President is working with the Department of Justice to ensure those involved will be identified and prosecuted. As this is an ongoing investigation, I cannot comment further, but rest assured, the President is confident in the investigation. PCRC is under the government's supervision and the security and the recovery teams will continue their vital work."

Scott: "What is the latest on the search for the fugitive Max Gold?"

Mr. Rose: "He is currently being sought. We are confident he has not left the state. He will be apprehended."

Scott: "The state has seen a tremendous amount of CCTV cameras being installed. On all major highways, in small towns, and inside government buildings. Also, new streetlights are being added to both urban and residential areas statewide. Are these new infrastructure upgrades solely for our safety?"

Mr. Rose: "The state has awarded a contract to the company Eye-Identify, which will provide these cameras and street lights to better assist the collection teams in spotting and retrieving infected persons before they can hurt themselves or others. These are no different than the cameras and sensors on the turnpike that track your tolls and monitor for speeding. This is all for the public's safety. Also, these are shovel-ready jobs. Many hardworking Americans are finding high paying jobs working on these camera installation projects. I don't hear any concerns coming from those well-paid workers. As these programs expand nationwide, so will the job opportunities for all Americans."

Scott: "We have not been able to find a website or any public information on this company Eye-Identify."

Mr. Rose: "You will need to ask them about their marketing efforts. I can provide you a contact for their office after the interview."

Scott: "*What is the extent of the authority of the PCRC contractors?*"

Mr. Rose: "As I stated, these are unprecedented times and have required unprecedented powers. The Contractor program has now been expanded to all states, which have experienced an outbreak. As a precaution the contractor program will soon be expanded to cover all 50 states. Although the Administration is confident the outbreak will be contained shortly, we don't want to take any risks."

Scott: "*Don't you mean 49, after all, Texas has succeeded and does not self-identify as part of the USA?*"

Mr. Rose: "There is an ongoing conversation between the Texas Governor and the President. I do not wish to discuss details at this moment, as these are sensitive negotiations. I do want to assure you though, that I have every confidence Texas will choose to remain part of United States of America."

Scott: "*The borders surrounding New Jersey have been partially reopened since their closure during the first forty-eight hours of the outbreak. How do you ensure no infected are getting past the checkpoints, either in or out of the state? Why not just evacuate all the residents until the virus can be contained?*"

Mr. Rose: "We have excellent border screening and vetting processes. We must look at the mortality risk-factor when deciding on a 'stay versus flee' plan. For example, in Japan, when the Fukushima nuclear reactor imploded, more people died due to the stress of being evacuated then died from radiation exposure. Right now, it is best if the residents of virus affected areas just shelter in place."

Scott: "You have said that, due to threats against the infected, the location of where they are being housed must be kept secret. Newly infected are being brought to these undisclosed locations. Many of the original infected are still housed on the college and university campuses throughout the state while awaiting relocation to these new, secret, Q-Zones. If a cure is not found soon, will loved ones be able to visit family members at these locations? If the infection continues, will these secret Q-Zones become overwhelmed? If so, to where will this growing population of infected be moved?"

Mr. Rose: "We hope very soon we will have all New Jersey colleges and universities re-opened. Displaced students have been offered positions with PCRC as contractors in order to earn money during this period. We anticipate all institutes of higher education to be fully sanitized and open for classes to resume shortly. The administration is in discussions with the university heads, and faculty, about how they can help speed up the process."

Clifford raised an eyebrow, but before he could fully digest what was said, Harry Rose continued talking.

"As for where the infected population is being housed currently, we have had to keep those locations a secret for the safety of the infected. There have been credible threats against them. Once the population is stable, and we see no further infections, or when a cure is implemented, visitation and hopefully release will soon follow."

Scott: "Please forgive the next question, but I have received it from dozens of reporters, it was the most frequently submitted question and the topic of internet buzz about zombies. Especially after videos surfaced of headless individuals still walking. I mean, no head at all. So, I must ask. Are the infected classified as living or dead?"

Mr. Rose: "The infected are very much living. They are suffering from an extreme form of Neonatal Progeroid Syndrome which prevents the infected from gaining weight, causing the body to digest all adipose tissue or body fat, giving them the skeletal appearance. This skeletal appearance has led to the term Skells. If the virus proceeds long enough in the host, the infected individual loses all mental capacity and will succumb to an addiction to human flesh. They are not attacking people for the sake of committing acts of violence. They simply cannot help themselves. They are like junkies who cannot stop their compulsions, no matter how harmful it is to themselves, or to others."

Scott: "And the reports of the infected experiencing mutations, particularly their stomach?"

Mr. Rose: "I must defer that question to the newly appointed Science Czar Doctor Woodrow Coleman. He is just getting settled in the administration and I am sure he will be available for interviews shortly."

Scott: "What about virus infected non-necrotic individuals, or VINNI's?"

Mr. Rose: "We have heard of some infected people who respond differently to the virus, although we do not have confirmed evidence of the type of individual of which you are referring. Again, the new Science Czar will be working closely with the CDC and HHS in evaluating these reports for validity."

Scott: "*When will President Callahan's wife, the first lady, return to New Jersey?*"

Mr. Rose: "The President's wife and children are currently touring military bases to show our armed services how important their service to our country is during this time of crisis."

Scott: "*Why is she visiting the US naval base in Guam?*"

Mr. Rose: "Each base is just as important as the next."

Scott: "*Guam?*"

Mr. Rose: "Yes. The US Naval base in Guam is important to the prior administration's pacific pivot. The current administration has not changed that focus."

Scott: "*Will the President move to the White House in Washington D.C.?*"

Mr. Rose: "Right now, New Jersey is ground zero of this pandemic and the president feels it is best for the nation that he stays here until this crisis is resolved."

Scott: "*The public has demanded a special election, so they can elect the new President. When will this occur? Several candidates from around the country have already begun positioning themselves to run.*"

Mr. Rose: "Let me make this perfectly clear, President Callahan IS the true President. This is called continuity of government and he was the last surviving official in the line of succession. As the only surviving elected official, he is the President. Yet he understands the concerns and will announce that a special election will be held very shortly."

Scott: "*We understand the President is going to run as neither Republican or a Democrat?*

Mr. Rose: "That is correct, he will run unaffiliated. He feels that the nation has been through enough and does not want to be divisive. He wants to show he is the President for Americans in all 50 states."

Scott: "49."

Mr. Rose: "ALL states. This is not a time for one's own self-interest. This is not a time for Americans political sides to focus on us against them. This is a time for national unity."

Scott: "Will the current administration abide by the outcome of the election if he does not win? He has his own private army within the PCRC ranks."

Mr. Rose: "The President, and the rest of the country, will abide by the outcome of any future election. There will be no challenge and there will be no claim of fraud or attempts to invalidate the outcome. The outcome is final."

Scott: "There is a rumor that the Anti-Trust division of the Department of Justice is investigating several US network news outlets to determine if they can be criminally charged for collusion. Meaning they are all working in concert with each other to deprive the consumer public with competitive content. This is a law that is usually brought against manufacturers or service providers, say insurance companies, to prevent them from working in concert with one another to keep the insurance rates high."

Mr. Rose: "I cannot comment on any ongoing investigation and we are not in charge of the DOJ, but I do understand the agencies concern."

Scott: "How could your administration see news outlets, which provide broadcast content free of charge, as denying the public access to competition?"

Mr. Rose: "I don't take these rumors about shutting down the media seriously, and again, it is the Department of Justice and they are a separate branch of government. But just for the intellectual exercise, let's look at your question. The information you provide as a news outlet is your product that you provide it to the public, do you not?"

Clifford nodded in agreement.

"And while the public does not need to tune into network television, they most likely will as it has become habit, much like using a cell phone. Follow me?"

Scott: "Yes, but we are providing the news free of charge. We are not charging them to watch the nightly news."

Mr. Rose. "But you are. Your network is supported by commercial advertising. Advertisers then pass those marketing costs on to their customers. So ultimately, the public is the one that is paying the costs for your broadcasts. The consuming public should have the right to access differing opinions and descriptions of the day's events. That way they can decide upon which network they choose to spend their time and advertising dollars. I am sure you agree with that, correct?"

Scott: "Umm, yes, that is true, but..."

Mr. Rose: "Let me finish. If those networks were secretly colluding to provide a unified, singular point of view while reporting on the day's events, thus depriving the public the ability to consume differing context, then yes, it would be considered collusion."

Scott was beginning to become flustered.

Scott: "So, let me ask, do you feel there is collusion between the major broadcast news outlets?"

Mr. Rose: "I am just talking hypothetically here, but collusion would only be true if the networks had misrepresented the relationships between one another. If the networks were publicly stating they are competitive, but secretly working together, in either an overt or tacit agreement, to present a singular, unified message, that reflected only a singular point of view, or perhaps singular bias, then they would be in collusion."

Scott: "Umm. So, you are saying..."

Mr. Rose: "I am just presenting a hypothetical for you. Let's say, for example, hypothetically, if all the entertainment reporters on all networks decided that they hated a film star by the name of John Smith. Then one night the reviewers from all the different networks get together at a cocktail party and discussed their mutual dislike for John Smith and that the film world would be better off without John Smith. You follow me?"

Scott: "Yes, I am following."

Mr. Rose: "After that private discussion, every mention of a movie starring John Smith is a scathing review. 'The worst movie that has ever stunk up a theater screen.' Well, that is not fair to the public, is it? The consuming public, the good people of the United States, are the ones that will miss out on great movie entertainment provided by John Smith. All because a small group of reviewers had colluded to torpedo any project he is attached to. Soon, the public will just stop liking John Smith and movie studios will stop hiring him."

Scott: "Ok, I understand your point about collusion of opinions, but news outlets don't report on opinions. They report on events and facts."

Mr. Rose: "How people view events and facts are not much different than how people view clouds in the sky. Some people look at a cloud in the sky and report that they see an elephant. Some may see a mountaintop or a train. Others will say they just see a cloud. Some of course see the cloud with a silver lining, and others just see storm clouds."

Scott: "Are you saying the administration feels the news media is colluding together to drive a single point of view about your administration, and thus, as you see it, is breaking the law and can be shut down?"

Mr. Rose: "Under no circumstances was I saying that. I was just speaking in hypothetical. I am confident that the networks, which use the public radio waves for their broadcasts, would never betray the trust of the people. After all, we all enjoy the freedom of looking up at the sky and seeing the clouds, don't we? Could you imagine what it would be like to spend the rest of your lifetime not being able to see the sky or the clouds?"

Scott: "Thank you for your time, Mr. Rose."

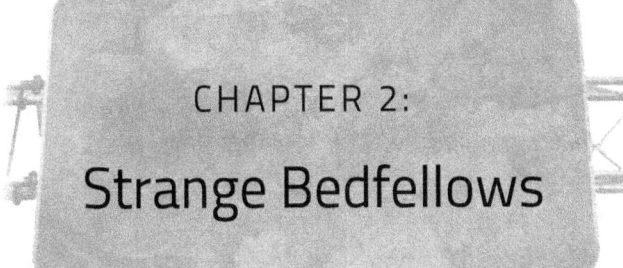

CHAPTER 2:

Strange Bedfellows

Ronan squeezed the tip of his nose, forcing the small, yellow, worm-like secretions from his pores. He was fascinated with the hotels 10x-magnifying mirror.

"There are worms living in my nose," he declared to Majesty, as he glimpsed the lower part of her body in the mirror.

"All I care about is that worm between your legs." Majesty replied. She lay in bed, gazing across the room at Ronan, as he stood naked in the bathroom.

She tossed the sheet off her own naked form and looked around the room. "I can't find my panties."

"I think I ate them." he replied, still basking in the after-glow of particularly satisfying sex.

"What is the plan? We need to strike again soon. We need to ensure they don't forget about us." Majesty said.

"We are going to strike again, but not yet, we need to show progress. We have done all that we can do with our violent methods. It is time we joined the political process." Ronan replied.

"Are you kidding me?" she asked incredulously. "What, you want to run for city council now?"

"No, I am not kidding. It is time we wipe the slate clean and find new tactics. We began this whole thing with the goal of trying to institute political change and we failed to even make a dent."

He strutted back to the bedroom, his junk swinging side-to-side "The government we had been fighting has consumed itself. The establishment is in tatters, but it has already begun to rise again from the ashes. It's time we also begin again and this time, do things differently." he said while sitting down at the foot of the bed.

"You're saying you want to be a politician now? Perhaps you should start by registering to vote first?" said Majesty in disgust.

"As if a single vote counts for shit." Ronan replied.

"Are you going to vote as a Democrat or Republican?" she joked.

"We are at the beginning of something new. Republican, Democrat, Socialist, Communist. Stop thinking in the past. We will vote for our own party, a new movement."

He stood up, faced her from the foot of the bed and grabbed each of her bare feet. He put his knees on the bed and crawled forward, raising her legs up into a widening V. "If I did vote, I would only vote for myself," he said.

"Why don't we just throw our support behind the green party?" she asked. "G.R.A.SS and the Greenie Weenies share a lot of the same slogans."

He positioned himself above her.

"Why don't we team with those pussies in the green party?" he replied, "Because I want to win, that's why. I said we are giving up the old ways. There are whole innovative ways of violence we have not yet even explored. I think I may allow you to try some out on me tonight," he said with an evil leer.

CHAPTER 3:

A Bellwether State

She did not ask him to buy her dinner. She was not hungry. Not for food anyway. She hadn't been hungry since she dropped the weight. All two hundred pounds of it, all in under twenty-four hours.

She had always been thick. 'Sturdy' was what her mom called her. 'Fat' was what her father called her. Bethany Obesity is what her bullies had called her in grade school.

She was alone, an outsider, an outlier of the norm. An anomaly among the kids who rated average on the body mass index.

The loneliness never left her as she grew into adulthood. She found friends and even the occasional lover as she entered her twenties, but she was still a big gal with high cholesterol and low self-esteem. Childhood insults leave scars that don't fade with time.

That all changed after she ate dinner at that high-end steak house in North Jersey. The next day, both she and the country began its metamorphosis.

She went alone, she did not want the judging looks from friends or co-workers while she powered down a plate full of beef. When she arrived at the posh eatery, the thin blond hostess in the micro black dress greeted her with a disdainful glare. 'Why would they want to greet their meat eating clientele with such an anemic looking waif?' she thought. This was a place to power down choice meats, and should have a hostess that reflected that philosophy. Not some gluten free, sugar free, carb free vegan who has not menstruated in five years.

She was seated at a table near the back. She ordered her meal as she caught a glimpse of the only other single person in the restaurant. A man, passionately enjoying a porterhouse. He radiated cholesterol and death.

Her own dinner was a great tasting, well marbled, cut of beef. A rare treat she would grant herself. A self-gift for her 28th birthday. Later that night, as she lay in bed suffering every type of intestinal discomfort and embarrassment imaginable, she listened to the sirens, screams and gunshots that rang out in her normally quiet suburb. She knew something was going down, but she was too sick to care. By the next night, her transformation was complete. She was a new person, physically anyway.

She lay low that night, not wanting anyone to see what she had become. Something she never imagined she could be. Lean and beautiful. She had no idea what to do in her new form. The news was filled with the Skell virus. The internet was filled with rumors of special Skells, those that were being specially sought out by the Contractors. Unique indi- viduals who had survived the virus, and had transformed into something new. The virus did not turn them into one of the emaciated zombies called Skells. This was either a different strain or perhaps the same strain that effected certain people differently. Those special people were no longer what they once were. They were altered biologically, genetically and psychologically. They could not be easily identified as infected without knowledge of that person pre- and post-infection. The change was startling. They were being referred to as Virus Infected Non-Necrotic Individuals or VINNI's. She knew she was a VINNI.

She felt beautiful. But she knew her friends and family would see her as a beast. They would know immediately that she was one of them. Would they turn her in? Would the government run experiments on her?

They were saying VINNI's were sick and could be dangerous. She felt fine. She did not feel homicidal or cannibalistic like the news reports said. She just felt...lonely.

She drove to her sister's house, taking with her nothing more than her laptop and the now ill-fitting clothes on her back. Her sister had been on vacation in Hawaii with her husband and teenage daughter when news of the virus broke. They were just beginning to let people back into the state, but her sister had posted online that they were choosing to stay on the island for a while longer. Bethany figured she had time to work things out and plan her next moves from her sister's empty home. Raiding her niece's closet, she tried on skin tight and revealing outfits in the full-length mirror.

There was a club down the street. Why not, she thought to herself? No one knew her in this area. She would dress up in one of the sexy outfits, sit at the bar, and experience what she never had before, the lustful attention of men.

She was not a virgin. She had been the recipient of some pity lays. Some drunken 'At 10 p.m. she's a two and at 2 a.m.

she's a ten' hook ups. Her first one was the worst. Freshman year of college, she went back to the dorm room with a drunken frat boy. He barely could get it up due to his drunkenness, and once he did, it was a double-pump-and-shoot session. He then fell asleep. She was too large a woman to lie comfortably in his bed, so she curled up on the open futon across the room. His roommate returned about an hour later and drunkenly threw himself on top of his sleeping friend. Not seeing her in the dark room, his curious roomy asked if he had scored that night.

The frat boy, believing she had already left, began to recount his night of elephant hunting, as he called it. He laughed as he recalled bagging a real porker. There were comments about slapping her ass and riding the waves, and rolling her in flour to find the wet spot.

She fled the room in tears and returned to her off-campus apartment.

She felt so pathetic and used, she cooked and ate by herself a frozen Italian dinner that was meant for four. Digging in through the low-grade chopped meat the white pasta shells in red sauce. She looked despondently at the ravaged tin pan, dented from where her fork had hit bottom and where she ripped the burned crust off the sides. She sat alone in her kitchen, dripping in sauce and shame.

But that was then, and this is now, and now she felt sexy. She was not sitting at the bar for more than fifteen minutes when the first man approached. There was some small talk. Some flirting. And then it was right back to her sister's place.

She had to learn how to have sex in this new body she inhabited. It was awkward at first, and the ability for her to actually be on top was exhilarating. It was fun, but in the end, it was not much different than the frat boy. Little foreplay, a few minutes of sex and once the condom was flushed away, a few seconds of pillow talk and he was asleep. She sat there, full of energy, while he snored, his pale, bare ass rising and falling with each deep breath he took.

That was the last clear memory she could recall, watching him breathe. She felt ill. Her pulse raced and her face flushed. Adrenaline was surging through her and she worried that she was having a stroke or a panic attack. She could feel the blood coursing inside her body, so loud it sounded like a freight train running through her veins. She could almost taste it. Her vision went red and she ran to the bathroom to be sick.

She woke up back on the bed staring at the ceiling. The bed beneath her was soaked. She did not remember leaving the bathroom. She began to recall bits and pieces of what had happened and sat straight up.

The memories were horrific. The biting, ripping, tearing, swallowing, eating, chewing, lapping, ripping, biting and chewing. The occasional crack of a bone.

The bed she had just shared with the stranger now resembled that ravaged tin pan of manicotti, the red splatter, the remnants of torn white pasta, and the lumps of unidentifiable meat. She had devoured the man so fast, she was not sure if he had even woken to scream.

But now, she felt fine again. She was herself again. Her new, thin, self.

She needed to investigate if others were experiencing this transformational phenomenon. She began an internet search upon all the hacker site blogs where she spent most of her evenings. Her normal haunts. Places where, until now, she had experienced her most satisfying anonymous relationships. It was then she noticed something not quite right with her system. As she fumbled with the mouse with her still blood-soaked fingers, the cursor briefly hovered over the Open-Apps icon. It indicated that there were four applications currently open on her system. She viewed only the three applications that she was aware of. She searched the desk for where she had previously put her glasses, only then realizing her vision, previously diminished by diabetic retinopathy, was once again a perfect 20/20. She checked the Open-Apps tool again.

The icon displayed that there were now only three applications open.

CHAPTER 4:

Third Party

Majesty walked past Ronan who was sitting attentively at his laptop, yet was still naked. The monitor displayed an attractive couple having aggressive sex.

"You pig!" she chastised him. "After what I just did to you, you're looking at this? Who is this slut?" Majesty snapped, her words dripping with annoyance and jealousy.

"This slut is a hacker. And pretty good one, but not smart enough to realize I had gotten around her self-coded security. For the past month, I have been able to track her every cyber movement, as well as non-cyber movement if it is in front of a camera." Ronan replied, proud of himself.

"Oh, and I am sure you only watch her for her hacking skills." Majesty hissed.

"This girl," Ronan replied while not taking his eyes off the screen, "was well over 300 pounds. At least she was as of 48 hours ago. In fact, she was so fat; I was amazed that she could use a keyboard so adeptly with her elephantine hooves. It seems my porcine friend here has had a massive weight loss. She literally dropped a ton overnight."

Majesty became interested. She was a lot of things. A revolutionary, a murderer, a feminist. But she was still a woman and if someone had a beauty or weight loss secret, she was all ears.

"I tracked her traffic and found she had been posting on a blog called 'Once Bitten'. It is a blog that appears to be a gathering place of people who had been bitten by Skells or infected with the virus in other ways. These bloggers, while still infected, had not yet turned into your typical brain dead, skin wrapped, cannibalistic walking skeletons we have come to know and love. In fact, the side effects are quite the opposite of life ending, but life renewing.

"All these people were once morbidly obese, and now they are slim, muscular and seem to be in good health, better than they ever were before the infection. They also seem to have little need for food. These are the rumored VINNI's we have been hearing about. Seems they are not a myth after all."

The couple on camera finished their sex and within minutes, heavy snoring came from the male.

"Who is prince snoring?" Majesty asked.

"No idea, I haven't seen him before. In fact, other than one chubby chaser she met on a fetish site, I don't think I have seen her ever bring home a man. I am assuming this is a random hook up to celebrate her newfound slimness. She probably posted an ad on that swiping app meant for sport fucking."

The woman on the video stood up, naked, and stumbled to the bathroom and shut the door. He heard the bathroom sink faucet turn on and water running in the sink. She must be going to take a piss and, ever the lady, hoping to block out the sound Ronan thought.

It didn't work. Niagara Falls would not have blocked out the sound that followed emanating from the bathroom.

"Holy cow." Majesty commented. "Find out where she ate dinner, I want to post a negative Yelp review."

The sounds made Ronan think back to his trip to Jordan. He was flying to Jordan via Oman to meet a famed Middle Eastern hacker. The airport had two terminals. Terminal A covered flights in and out of Europe, America and Asia and hosted all the top tier airlines. It was stunning, with lavish shops and restaurants catering to the well-heeled international traveler. Kiosks selling the finest fabrics and handmade jewelry and even a vending machine that dispenses gold bars like candy.

Terminal B was on the other side of the airport but may have well been the other side of the world. Terminal B was where low-cost airlines would transport migrant workers who dug the ditches, poured the concrete and swept the streets, outside in temperatures hotter than the surface of the sun. Piss poor, third world nationals, carrying their meager belongings in plastic shopping bags, returning to whatever armpit of a failed nation they came from. If there was a hell on earth, these poor creatures were living it.

He found himself stuck in Terminal B waiting on a delayed flight out of Oman, and regretting the hummus and spiced meat dinner he had eaten an hour earlier.

He made his way to the men's room. It was at that moment, after decades of trying to bring America down, when he finally he realized how good he had it. If for nothing else other than the sanitary conditions of public accommodations. The Omani airport terminal bathroom had three stalls to choose from. Two contained regular, eastern style toilets. The one in middle was just a hole in ground that the user would squat over and lets the turds free-fall into the abyss.

This stall was for those Terminal 2 patrons that were unac-customed to the finer things in life, such as indoor plumbing. In the first toilet stall, an airport worker was explaining in one language how to work the seated toilet to a migrant who spoke an entirely different language.

Ronan grabbed the only remaining stall equipped with a toilet. He sat down and began taking care of business, when, of course, someone entered the middle stall.

He heard it all. The sounds would forever be seared into his mind.

The blasts. The shit logs that failed to directly hit their target hole, and instead splatted on the floor. The grunts as the man tried to keep his balance in this sick version of lawn darts.

Then the guy used a nearby hose to clean out his anal orifice. Their version of toilet paper.

Ronan shuddered and wished for a memory wipe.

He was brought out of this horrible memory with the sound of a thud. The woman he was watching on the laptop had fallen to the ground, hard. A second thud as if she fell again against the bathroom door. Majesty leaned in, also curious as to what was happening on the live feed.

The bathroom door opened a bit, closed, and then swung open wide. The woman ran from the bathroom and pounced on her sleeping lover. She began biting him viciously, ripping chunks of meat out of his back. The man awoke and tried to struggle, but she forced him down onto the bed to finish her meal. He was dead in minutes as she continued her feeding frenzy.

Majesty ran into her own bathroom to hurl.

The webcam girl slowed her eating, and, as if she was coming out of a dream, looked around realizing the horrific scene surrounding her. She backed away from the bloody mess, horrified, then looked down at her own blood covered naked body, and ran from the room.

"Interesting." Ronan said out loud to himself. "Was that a delayed response to the virus, or was it triggered by the sex?"

"Honey," he called out to Majesty, but she was busy blowing chunks. "I think I found my constituency."

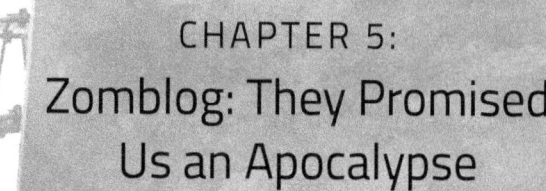

CHAPTER 5:
Zomblog: They Promised Us an Apocalypse

Attention Posters, please review the pinned message at the top of this blog. Please follow the rules to keep this blog spam, troll and Skell free. Be respectful, no flaming, no off-topic postings and no selling of anything. Violators will have their posts deleted and repeat violators will be banned from the group. This blog is to discuss the current, slow moving, zombie virus outbreak. The Zombie Apocalypse sure ain't what they sold us in movies and T.V. Now have fun and share your experiences. Thank you. —*Zomblog moderator*

So today, I found an arm on the sidewalk in front of my house. A human arm! A fucking human arm! There were no other body parts anywhere to be seen and no signs that an attack took place right on that spot which would have caused this dismemberment. WTF???

All I can think was that some fucking Skell was creeping around my house, and in such a ragged condition, his arm just fell off and he kept shambling onward. When is the government going to do something about these creatures? The streets aren't safe day or night. I can't even let my dog go out and play in the back yard alone anymore. My neighbor's cat has been missing for three days. You know that thing ain't coming home. Cat chow now. —*Angry Man*

I hear you Angry Man. Getting a child off to school every morning is now a coordinated military operation. Now that schools are back open, there are still the normal activities we moms put up with every morning. We make sure the lunches are packed, that they wearing the right clothes? Do they have gym class or band practice that day? Is the homework finished and put away? It was a struggle to keep up before the zombie apocalypse began.

Now before I walk them to the bus stop, I must go through my own checks. Is my gun fully loaded? Is my phone with the WALKR app fully charged? Are there any Skell sightings in my neighborhood this AM? We moms bear the burden. —*Mommy needs a Drinky*

I hate that I can no longer just walk out of my house anymore. You must look out the windows to be sure the yard is clear of Skells before you open the door. You cannot even open the garage door anymore, as it takes too long for the door to roll down and close. Those creatures can be fast if they see you. My neighbor was chased into his garage. He made it to the back to push the close button, but by the time the slow-moving door came down, two of them zombies made it inside. He got into his house ok, but then had those two flesh eaters banging around in his garage, getting blood and bile and shit all over his wife's brand-new Lexus. Took nearly thirty minutes before the PCRC recovery team showed up to retrieve and cart them away. What the hell am I paying my taxes for? —*Golfing Fool*

I feel so bad for them. I want to help, and change people's perceptions about them. What these zombies, or Skells, or whatever you call them, need is a good hash tag campaign. I have not seen a good one that espouses the cause of the infected. I was thinking of launching a couple to see what sticks. #LIFE or Life is For Everyone. Or #SkellLove or #Fight-4Infected. What do you think? Can a hash tag be trademarked? —*SixtiesinSpirit*

What they need is a bullet in the head! #SkellKiller #Skell=Hell —*Anonymous.*

That won't do anything, I have seen one or two with most of their head missing, and still walking. You must gut them. That is the only way to stop them. Not kidding. You need to remove their entire stomach. #MustGutThem —*Roadkill*

This is a conspiracy, I tell you. This is a government scam to keep us frightened and compliant. I heard that they are not real zombies, but actors dressed up. And those trucks that pick them up, just take them to other areas to be dropped off. I am telling you, this is all a hoax! —*AntMan*

Hey AntMan, I don't agree with you that this is a hoax, as two of my coworkers were killed and several members of my church have become infected and I know they are not part of any acting troop and would not participate in any type of hoax. But I do think you are on to something about the infected being dropped off. I also heard tales that after the collection trucks pick up the infected, they simply go dump them in another part of town and then collect them again the next day. I thought it was pure BS, but then I saw something very weird.

Last Sunday, we came out of church and found four infected in the parking lot. It was a real scare, I'll tell you. But what made it worse was one of them was Sue Wells, the gal who runs the day care center. She was all dressed up with a pink sweater, as if she may have been on her way to church that morning when she was attacked. Well we all took out our phones and used that Skell reporting app and sure enough, the white truck showed up, collected them with those long polls and carted them off. It was darn traumatic for the congregation to witness that.

Well, a few days later, I was visiting my sister upstate and realized that I would not be able to get home before the curfew went into effect. So, I planned to bed down there that night and as I was helping my sister put out the garbage on the front curb, sure as sugar, there is Sue Wells shambling down the street. Still wearing that pick sweater. It was her, no doubt about it. And this was a good seventy-five miles from where they collected her days earlier. Did she escape? If she did, how did she make it all the way up there? Just weird. —*Man in god's plan*

It's called managing risk perception; they are trying to convince us that this is spread further than it is. Perhaps they are driving around dropping off infected into regions to punish communities that are not obeying curfew? —*Bush Can Man*

It's called fucked up, that's what it is! —*AntMan*

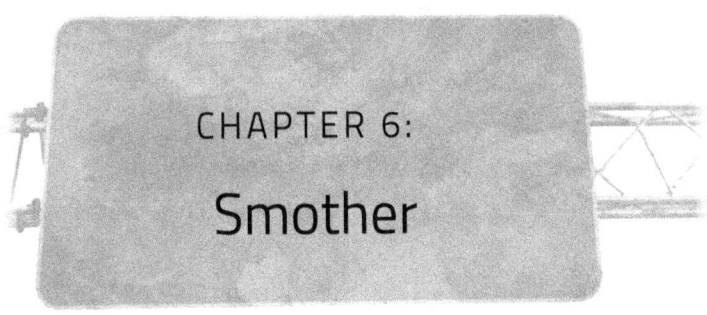

CHAPTER 6:

Smother

"There's not much time now," she said as her fingers gently touched the sides of his face.

"Not much time left," the voice repeated, speaking as much to herself as she was to him. Her voice was soft and sad in intonation.

"Not much time left," she said again.

Her presence and voice were there, but she was not.

Phantom fingers caressed his cheeks as they moved in unison towards his mouth.

"He's coming," she said again, her tone becoming more determined.

"Wh...what?" Ivan muttered, not yet awake.

Her fingers approached his lips and interlocked over his mouth.

"Mmmph," Ivan murmured confused and concerned.

Her fingers flattened across of his mouth, her hand shifted, placing her left palm flatly over his lips. Her right hand laid atop her left hand and together the two hands pushed downward, his head sinking into the pillow.

Ivan stirred.

The voice was a loud whisper. "He's coming, there's not much time now."

The woman's palms covered his mouth and nose completely. His body was still, as if paralyzed, but his head jerked up and down. Her hands ensuring that he received no further oxygen.

Ivan leaped forward, gasping for air and swinging his arms at emptiness in the dark room.

"Ivan?" Marifi said, sleepily and concerned. He did not answer.

"You have sleep apnea." Marifi said, awoken from her own dreams by Ivan's near nightly convulsions.

"No, this was different." Ivan responded, sitting up in the bed, staring straight forward, ensuring each breath filled his lungs before exhaling.

"You have to pee? Don't pee the bed!" she said. He could not tell if she was joking or not.

"My mother. She was smothering me. The same dream again."

"That was a long time ago, she's gone now. Go back to sleep." Marifi consoled.

"Strange that her attempted murder of me is one of the few remaining memories I have of her." Ivan lamented.

"Your family is dysfunctional." Marifi said, stumbling a bit on that last word. Ivan found it adorable.

"Where is he?" Ivan asked.

"You don't need to see him right now." she warned.

"I do," he insisted.

"He's in the game room, but I am going with you." she said.

"No, I want to see him alone. He won't hurt me. He can't anymore." Ivan said as he threw off the covers.

Ivan walked down the hallway the game room; a haughty name for what was just an area in the bunker with a large screen TV and enough games and extra consuls to last a nuclear winter half-life. As he entered, an X-Box controller flew past his face and slammed against the wall. His father Max stood there, angry his throw missed its intended target.

"Let me out of this fucking dungeon," Max demanded.

"If I let you out, they will kill you." Ivan replied, picking up the controller and replacing the batteries that had flown loose.

"Lots have people have wanted to kill me over the years. Business partners, competitors, your wife. Even you, I'm sure. I don't need protection, especially from you." Max spat.

"This is different. You are a wanted man now," Ivan explained. "You're being hunted by G.R.A.SS because of your foaming program; and hunted by your own contractors who have laid all the blame for the program at your feet. Hunted by the public who now knows you were the architect of this generation's 'final solution' for the Skells, and who believe you were most likely the father of the virus itself. Shall I go on?" Ivan asked.

Ivan placed the controller down near the TV. "My father, a Jew, heading a program to funnel the sick and unwanted into a chamber for suffocation. We really come full circle as a people."

Max raged. "I don't need to hear your sanctimonious bullshit. I have had to hear about your nonsense ideas for the past decade. Burning through the money I put aside for you, by building luxury doomsday shelters. How fucking ridiculous is that? You couldn't just go and sell real estate, you had to go and try to sell life after death, like some evangelical radio con-man." Max sneered.

"And what did you think was going to happen, even if, for once in your life, you were successful? Let's say you found enough idiots to buy your underground condos. Then the apocalypse hits. How long do you think your moron tenants would keep their sanity down there? They would turn into savages, no matter how much you tried to wrap them in luxury like pampered children. You think bowling alleys; video games and memory foam mattresses would keep them distracted from the knowledge that it's all gone on the outside? Knowing that everyone else is dead and there is nothing to return to topside?!" Max yelled.

"And who the hell would keep the place running? You would need an army skilled manual labor types to keep that kind of place functional. How long would it be before the cooks, cleaners and garbage workers turn on those pampered assholes? Christ, I can't even keep a Mexican gardener on the payroll for more than six months before he's asking for a raise. You think you could control an entire stratified society in your doomsday cocoons? You think the working-class inhabitants were merely going to stay in their servant roles? I wouldn't give it two months before they slit your tenant's throats while they slept on their hypoallergenic pillows!"

Ivan tried to interject but Max was not having it.

"Just keep your fucking mouth shut and listen to me Ivan. I have worked my whole life so that we could limit our exposure to those types of people. They say this country is a melting pot. That is bullshit. I don't care how much blending there is.

It's culture that separates us. It's not color, nor wealth or religion. Its culture, and distinct cultures don't congeal. Culture is
what will keep us on top of this world, not living underground
in some fantasy human ant farm you have concocted." Max
finished his sermon and took a deep breath.

Ivan sat motionless for a moment. He collected his
thoughts. He began twice to speak, only to catch himself. He
was not going to sink to that level. It's true; all sons become
their father eventually. But not today.

"And yet," Ivan slowly and calmly began, "here you are.
Here with me. All your efforts. All your hard work and sacrifice.
All the best laid plans, and you end up down here, under-
ground, in one of the human ant farms I created."

"You forced me down here. I would rather die than live
here." Max snapped.

"We have no intention of having you live here with us."
Ivan said.

"Marifi and I discussed it. As soon as we can, we will provide
you safe passage to a private airport where a pilot who does
not know who, or what, you are, has been instructed to fly
you out of the state. He has been paid to take you anywhere
within the United States. He will not return, so I will never
know where you tell him to take you. I don't care where you
go, but you will be gone, and if you are found, your imprisonment or death won't be on our hands."

"You're letting me go?" Max asked in disbelief.

"I have no desire to see you dragged into the streets
and murdered by an angry mob. And I didn't want to see you

arrested by your own contractors. I am giving you a fighting chance to escape." Ivan said though gritted teeth.

"Well what are you waiting for, take me now!" demanded Max.

"We have not yet finished our business transaction." Ivan replied. "As I told you in your office, there is still the matter of owed past allowance. You have missed many, many years of payments. I think one million dollars in crypto currency should cover it. You know, if I add in all the Bitcoins the tooth fairy should have left under my pillow."

"So, that's what this is about. *My money*. You want money!" Max exclaimed Bribery, kidnaping and extortion were concepts he could work with, and he for the first time, felt a tinge of pride in Ivan for going that route. "If you had just made that clear in the beginning, we could have avoided all this daddy issue nonsense." Max said.

"But then we would have missed this precious time together." Ivan sneered.

"I can get you the money, just let me have access to a computer, I can transfer over to you in minutes." Max said in full bargaining mode with his captor.

"No computers here. We are up against a very sophisticated cyber opponent in G.R.A.SS. Once you log on to the internet, from any computer, they will immediately know it is you. They will find this location and they will kill us. All of us. You may find death preferable than this bunker, but Marifi and I intend to stay alive. I have heard that people are being rounded up, and not just the zombies. Anyone above ground is an easy target."

"Then let me go use a computer somewhere safe. I will put on a disguise. I am an old man, what am I going to do, run away from you? Overpower you? I can't give you cyber currency without a computer!"

Ivan leaned back in his chair. "We will head to the public library first thing in the morning. If you don't do anything stupid, you can use the computer there, make the transaction, and as soon as I am sure the money is secured in my account, we will take you to the airport." Ivan offered.

"A public library, what do I look like, the homeless?" Max sneered.

"Well, technically you are homeless." Ivan reminded him.

"Take me to an internet café." Max offered.

"I built a bunker, not a time machine. There are no internet café's anymore. It's the public library or nothing." Ivan said, enjoying the tables being turned.

"Fine, the public library." Max relented. "I will be sure not so shower so I fit in with the rest of the filth and pedophiles there."

"Good chat, Dad." Ivan said as he began to leave, then stopped and snapped his fingers like he had forgotten something. "Oh yeah, one more request, when we get there, and before I give you access to the world-wide web, I want you to answer a question for me that I've had since I was a child."

"Yeah," Max said suspiciously. "And what is that?"

"Just out of curiosity, why did you kill mom?"

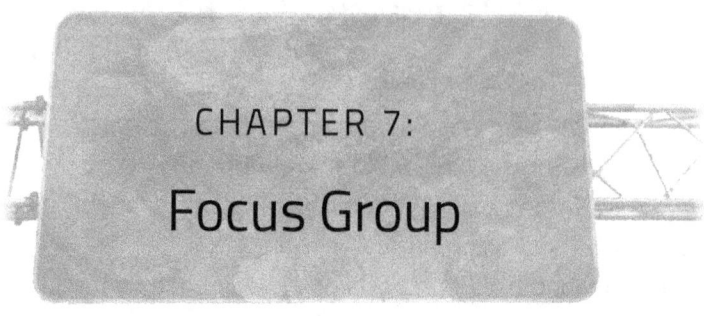

CHAPTER 7:

Focus Group

They were a diverse bunch, brought together to weave a tapestry of modern American society. Each person, chosen after thorough review to make up a broad, cross-section of the country. They all represented a different race, religion, gender, ethnicity and political philosophy. They were black, white, yellow and brown; as well as a fairground color wheel combination of skin tones that resulted from generations of multicultural humping.

Young and old, educated and ignorant, doctors and ditch diggers, bible thumpers and sport humpers.

The only thing they had in common was they were free on a Sunday afternoon to participate in a focus group with the promised payment of a one hundred dollar Target gift card for their time and opinions.

Triston was the group facilitator representing Autumn Marketing LLC. He stood in front of them, iPad in hand, reading off the pre-chosen questions. Data sets which, would then be synthesized and grouped into abstractions. Concepts and paradigms would then be formulated. Finally, a profile would present itself. This marketing firm was trying to find the perfect man or woman to lead their cause. And the job of identifying the correct profile of persons, fell to Autumn Marketing LLC, and its parent organization, G.R.A.SS.

Questions were asked such as:

What are you looking for in a political leader?

What is more important, what a leader says or how a leader makes you feel?

Where do you find information in order to make your voting decision?

The questions were not much different than run of the mil political polling.

It was after lunch was served that the questions became more targeted, more personal. Attendees were asked to submit their answers via a provided computer tablet as to keep the replies anonymous and uninfluenced by others in the room.

Have you ever known someone, other than a family member, that you would willingly die for? Please describe.

Have you ever known someone, other than a family member, that you would willingly kill for? Please describe.

Is it possible to truly love and worship someone you have never personally met?

Who do you hold accountable for the Skell virus outbreak?

When you heard that the infected were being exterminated through foaming, how did you feel; relieved or appalled?

Do you believe the infected are living or dead?

Have you put down any Skells?

What are your feelings of people who have survived the infection, but did not succumb enough to become a Skell, otherwise known as Virus Infected Non-Necrotic Individuals, or VINNI's. Should they be released or should they be held for further study?

Do you feel the new curfews, restrictions and laws enacted during the Skell outbreak have gone too far, are reasonable to provide safety, or have not gone far enough to protect the public?

What are your feelings about Texas seceding from the United States? Should military action be taken to bring them back into the USA or good riddance?

As the questioning came to an end, Triston gave a nod towards the two-way mirror where he knew Marcus, Joel and Shoshanna were munching on gluten free, vegan snacks and sipping fair-trade wine. He knew they had gathered all the information that Ronan had requested and it was time to end the focus group.

He thanked the assembled group for their time and walked out the door on the right side of the room.

The group sat in silence for a moment, drained of information and sleepy from the pizza lunch.

"You know; they really did not ask any questions about the Trans community." said the thick rimmed glasses wearing, heavily tattooed brunet who was there to represent millennial females.

"Hey!" yelled out the man with the beer belly who represented the working-class white. "Where's our goddamn gift card?!"

The double doors on the left side of the room opened and the Skells came marching in.

In the observer area, Triston and the others reviewed the results of the question and answer session, undistracted by the scene taking place on the other side of the mirror. A pro-choice soccer mom stood alongside a lesbian who leans Republican in their attempt to pull a rampaging Skell off a blood-soaked lawyer, who was raised Jewish but self-identifies as Episcopalian. Meanwhile the proverbial angry black woman was swinging her chair fending off two former sorority sisters, who were now infected and emaciated flesh eaters. An Asian male libertarian and a Hispanic woman, who publicly stated her support of the Green Party but was secretly a humanist who had never voted, pounded on the door seeking a rescue that would not come.

Triston was about to suggest to his marketing team that they call it a day so that he could make his evening hot yoga class the exit door burst open.

"Get down!" yelled the first man entering the room. He was clad in a black tactical uniform. This shouted command was followed by more men entering, yelling, shooting and the sound of Shoshanna shrieking.

By the time 7322 entered the room, it had been fully secured and all threats posed by man, or Skell had been neutralized.

CHAPTER 8:

Chum

van, Marifi and Max walked into the public library across from a university that was still being disinfected after serving as an infected holding area for the past month.

They made their way towards an empty row of bolted to the table laptop computers. Ivan stealthily slipped masking tape over the webcam before he nodded for Max to sit in front of the keyboard.

Ivan slipped another piece of tape over the webcam of the adjacent laptop and sat down next to his father. Marifi stood behind Max.

"OK, now here's the situation." Ivan explained to Max. "There are a lot of very clever people looking for both of us. People who know how to use the internet for more than sharing family photos and searching for porn. They have very powerful analytics software which is swimming up and down the cyber rivers looking for keywords that only the likes of you or I would search. Facial recognition programs running in the cloud that are searching webcams statewide that can identify both us, even while wearing a disguise."

Max looked at Ivan, and then up at Marifi, noticing she had left her sword in the car. Ivan was also unarmed, though he was worthless with a gun even when he had one. Max glanced around the immediate area seeking something that could be used as a weapon should the opportunity present itself.

Ivan continued. "So, don't be obvious when you go online. Don't open any of your email accounts. Don't remove the tape from the webcam, as it will take only seconds to identify you and your location. All you are going to do is access one of your crypto accounts, and move the currency into the account number I provide you. Understood?"

"Understood." Max replied.

The two men paused. Marifi could almost feel the hate radiating between them.

"Wonderful." Ivan exclaimed as he slapped both his hands on his thighs with the fakest of smiles. "But we need to ensure you do not attempt anything funny, so, I am going to need to restrain you. I hope you understand. Ivan said with a smirk. "And please Dad, don't draw any attention to yourself, we wouldn't want that would we?" Ivan said with a satisfied grin across his face.

Max felt his left wrist being pulled down and heard the click of handcuffs securing him to the leg of the chair. Another click and his leg was secured to the table. He looked up at Marifi with a death glare as she rose back up.

"Now one last thing," Ivan continued, drawing the old man's attention away from Marifi. "Since we will never see or speak to each other again after today, I need to ask you one question and I want a simple answer. That question is 'Why'?"

Max leaned forward in his chair

He had spent his lifetime using people as currency. His success came from a lifetime of treating human beings as a venture capitalist treated startup companies. If he saw a spark of possibility that his investment of time and money in a person would pay dividends later in life, he continued cultivating. If they did not pan out, he was quick to cut and run.

It was a winning formula that, until recently, went undetected by any of the lives he had manipulated.

It was important that his investments would not stray from the path Max set. He removed anything that could alter their trajectory, mainly the subject's fathers. Max had arranged the imprisonment, abandonment and untimely deaths of many men, so that their sons and daughters would grow up, loyal and dedicated to the only man in their life, Max.

As years went by, he realized the younger the subject, the more successful he was at fully manipulating their lives for his personal gain. So, he had a child of his own to provide him a gateway to new candidates. As a child Ivan had borne witness to Max's focus and manipulation of these children's lives.

Max took a deep breath, he had been waiting for this day.

"Ok," he began. "Let's just be honest with each other. After all, once your son is old enough to kidnap you; he is a man, and thus old enough to know the facts of his own life. First off, let me start with your so-called wife. I am sure by now you know about the arrangement? She was identified for her unique combination of beauty and lethality. Much like many of the assets I have cultivated over the years, she too has been bred to kill.

"We found her, we brought her here, and we fooled you into thinking you meeting her was accidental and that she wanted to marry you. You were so desperate for someone to love you that you never questioned how a woman like her would fall for a *man* like you.

"Has she told you all the details of how we bartered the life of her beloved grandfather in exchange for her compliance? How if she didn't follow the plan, we would share his whereabouts with the Philippine terror group from which he had fled? They too had invested in her father since he was a child, training him to become a butcher of men, and would not have treated him kindly had they found him. Their torture of choice is to peel off the skin from their living victims. A torture I believe your wife has some familiarity with. I hear she used it to secure your escape from Pinskey's men? I choose her well." Max sneered at Ivan.

"Did she also tell you that if you, my son, were to ever become a danger to me; that she would be given an order to kill you? Did she tell you she agreed to these requirements of her employment? One text from me and she would have slit your throat."

Ivan turned to his bride, and gave her an exaggerated wink. "Impressive my love," he said. "I hope you would have at least made me a final meal before my execution."

Marifi gave no response. She grew up in a society where children revered their elders and cared for them till they day they died. Even the terrorists loved their mothers and fathers. Siblings and cousins and second cousins never moved far from each other and multiple generations of the same family lived under the same roof. She could not understand America, where adult children see their parents only as a bank or a burden, and giving a LIKE on a Facebook post was considered staying in touch. But the Gold family was beyond anything she could have ever imagined.

Max turned to Marifi. "This would have been a time for that kill-order to come down. But don't worry young lady. Your father won't be harmed due to your failure to meet your obligations. He died on his own about three months ago. Alcohol abuse I believe. Liver failure. I am sure it was not a peaceful or pain free end to his life. Perhaps it was knowing what a burden he had become to his only known grandchild, that he could not help but to drink himself to death. So, young lady, since you are of no further use to the corporation, you can consider our arrangement and your employment now terminated."

The news of her grandfather's death struck Marifi with a physical jolt. She seemed to wilt slightly, her eyes drifted off.

Max turned his attention back to Ivan. "Son, the primary fact is this after a lifetime of success, you are my only failure. You are my ultimate disappointment."

This revelation was not exactly news to Ivan.

Max continued. "Once we began our stem cell research, I thought that it could be you who held the key. When your friend Woodrow stumbled upon the Modified Embryonic Animal Tissue concept, I truly believed it would be your stem cells that we could harvest to develop the MEAT, and the virus. That it would be your voice that would control the infected. Try as we did, we could not make the process work with you as the host."

Max grinned.

"You truly are a failure, right down to the cellular level." Max laughed.

Ivan was determined not to react.

"The only purpose you ever served was to draw together more suitable subjects for purposes. I used you so that I could identify the more useful. You were bait. No, bait is too strong a term. If I were a fisherman, you would not even qualify as bait."

"You were chum!"

"I used you to chum the waters and draw in those more suitable for my future use.

"Your mother knew of my disappointment in you. She knew of my disappointment in her for producing such a failure.

"Women get used to a certain standard of living. She feared losing what I had provided her. You wouldn't understand that. Your wife came from nothing, married nothing, and now has nothing. She follows you from one underground burrow to another.

"She attempted to kill you, yes. But not to protect you from me. She was looking to protect herself. She feared I would leave her, and attempted to erase her mistake. When I found her mid act, I tried to stop her, but the wrong person died."

"If you have something to say, say it, but now you know the truth." Max finished, letting out a long cathartic breath.

Marifi could see the impact on Ivan. It was subtle, something only she, and perhaps Max could spot in him. Max's words had fractured him. It was a subtle change in Ivan's face, like the shifting of a tectonic plate, hundreds of miles below the surface of the earth. Undetectable to the human eye. He was unrecognizable to her now.

Ivan sat silent, motionless, expressionless, looking at his father.

Ivan finally displayed a weak smile.

"Thank you for being honest with me." Ivan said icily. "Now, let's get you online and complete our business here."

Ivan stood up and ripped the tape from the webcam.

"Wait! What the hell are you doing?!" Max yelled.

"We drained your bitcoin account yesterday. Just sit back and smile for your selfie." Ivan said coldly. Without a glimpse back at his father he turned on his heel and disappeared through the exit with Marifi following at his heels.

Max tried to get up to follow them but was unable. He thrashed and the chair fell to the ground. He shouted in pain from the cuffs digging into his wrist. He yelled for the woman behind the counter, but she was busy on the phone with 911.

"Who do you think will get to him first?" Marifi asked Ivan as they made their way to the car, leaving Max's profanity riddled shouts in their wake.

"Who cares, as long as they keep him alive long enough to see his favorite adopted son die." Ivan replied, his mind set on settling one final score.

Assassinating the President.

CHAPTER 9:
The Hunter, the Soldier, and the Shepherd

7322 sat in his office reviewing the documents collected during the raid on Autumn Marketing and G.R.A.SS.

He pieced together what they had been up to. Autumn had assembled a focus group to test the public's reaction on messaging. The messaging was to be delivered by G.R.A.SS leader Ronan Campbell. As 7322 flipped through the notes, they read like traditional political party position papers and talking points. How to introduce a candidate, and what buzzwords and slogans would resonate with the base. Politics 101.

The second part of the binder contained evidence more ominous. Autumn had been assembling profiles on individuals. Candidates that were being considered for filling a bizarre job description.

7322 knew G.R.A.SS was lethal, but he saw them all as amateurs. A group of disparate troublemakers with an overarching theme of upending the status quo. Typical, run of the mill, wannabe anarchists. Analysis of the members that had been captured or killed showed that the group most likely would burn out on its own soon.

Most of the identified members came from upper middle-class backgrounds. Hackers whose activity in the group consisted of denial of service attacks on government and corporate websites, and whose physical violence did not extend much beyond smashing Starbucks windows and burning SUV's.

They were known as terror-tourists. White, suburban teens to twenty-somethings who would eventually grow out of their youthful angst or quit once they felt frightened by the real violence. For most, it was a pit stop before realizing they wanted a nice house, car and 401K more than they wanted a revolution.

G.R.A.SS had never been viewed as an apocalyptic death cult. Yet the recovered documents made it clear they were heading in that direction. The goal was to turn the country into a wasteland. They were so confident that the end was near that they were evaluating future post-apocalyptic leaders.

What shook 7322 to his core was that he personally knew a couple of the candidates listed in the G.R.A.SS dossiers. He himself was listed as a front-runner.

These cyber psychos had a full profile on him, including his secret likes and interests that only someone monitoring his private online searches would be aware of.

7322 realized he was no longer alone in his office, President Patrick Callahan had quietly entered and was hovering in front of him.

"I heard the raid was successful." Patrick commented flatly.

7322 quickly rose to his feet while simultaneously closing the binder.

"Yes sir, it was. We suffered no casualties, unfortunately though we were only able to rescue two civilian captives. Several G.R.A.SS members were on site. They resisted and were killed. All but one, who is in the infirmary now with non-life-threatening injuries."

"That is a shame." Patrick replied.

With the complete absence of context, 7322 could not tell if Patrick felt it was 'a shame' that several of the suspects had died or that one had survived.

"I was told some valuable intelligence has been found?" Patrick asked.

7322 seethed, as it was his role to brief the president. Some asshole had circumvented his authority and already briefed the President on details. "Yes sir. I planned on reviewing and providing you a full summary as soon as we can figure out what it all means."

Patrick reached forward and removed the binder from 7322's tight grip. He began flipping through it casually.

"Nutshell it for me." Patrick requested.

7322 grew nervous. He did not want the President seeing his own profile listed. Would Patrick think that he was collaborating with G.R.A.SS?

The President was not the man who took office just a short while ago. Those close to him had noticed he had become more erratic and irritable. He was barely sleeping and had lost a great deal of weight. Patrick had been refusing to eat anything that was not 100 percent plant based and demanded he watch, as all his meals were prepared. He was spiraling into paranoia and isolation.

"Well Mr. President, the unusual part is that the group was preparing for the end of the world. Now, taken in context, there have always been apocalyptic cults predicting our species demise. The only differentiator between them is the *how*. Whether they are preaching that we are about to get snuffed out by god, or by aliens, by global warming or an artificial intelligence singularity." 7322 said with a sarcastic tone to lighten the mood.

"Or the zombie apocalypse." The President replied, in a strange and dull monotone.

"Well yes, people are susceptible to whatever is currently trending as the biggest threat to mankind. In the fifties, it was aliens. In the sixties, nuclear war, the seventies it was the coming ice age. And in the eighties, we thought MTV would bring about Armageddon." 7322 noticed the Presidents right eye twitched involuntarily and realized he should probably stop with the jokes.

"So," 7322 continued tentatively. "It appears that G.R.A.SS was searching for someone who could rise-up and become a leader in the groups imagined, post-apocalyptic, America. They had quite a lineup of contenders. The American Idol of the Apocalypse."

"And?" Patrick probed further.

"Well, it appears that...well...some of those evaluated were from your inner circle. Non-other than Daniel Sullivan, who has been working with me and I know is absolutely loyal to the administration. No reason to assume he was even contacted. I am guessing they were looking at people with proximity to you. Also, there was Colonel James Tindall."

"Why do I know that name?" Patrick looked up from his reading.

"Troubling story, unfortunately. Years ago, the Colonel was running covert intelligence operations overseas. He caught wind that the prior administration was arranging a prisoner swap. We were giving away three highly dangerous biophysicist that were being held in GITMO. These three were in exchange for one of our own soldiers who was being held by the Taliban.

"Even the Pentagon was concerned about this swap, as the captive soldier was a traitor. The only reason we would bring him home was to court martial his ass. Not worth releasing three men who had advanced, bio-terror capabilities. Yet the prior administration was very eager to get those scientists out of GITMO, so we announced the trade.

"Colonel Tindall had voiced his concerns right up to the President. But, the White House told Colonel Tindall to drink a tall glass of 'shut the fuck up', but he continued poking around and inquiring about the prisoner swap.

"So, the White House 'accidentally' ousted the Colonel." 7322 said making air quotes with his fingers. "They accidently released his information and the role he served overseas. While they quickly pulled the information back and claimed it was a 'mistake', his cover was blown and he was hustled out of country and out of his command. He was demoted and buried in a new role at Fort Detrick. Turns out the Colonel was right to be concerned, because those scientists never made it back to their home counties. They were scooped up by PCRC and put to work on the MEAT project. It appears that the whole prisoner swap story was a smoke screen to get these guys out of GITMO and into the PCRC labs."

"Jesus Christ." Patrick said with disgust at what his own government could do to their military personnel. "Isn't this the guy who was given command of the Princeton Q-zone?" he asked, referring to forward operating base Brains.

"Yes sir, he is currently on the run, but we are confident we have tracked he and his followers down." 7322 assureds.

"OK, and who else was on the list?" Patrick asked.

7322 decided to leave out that his own name had been thrown in the hat and skipped to the next name "The next name was really an odd choice. They had a profile on Max Golds son Ivan. Ivan Gold is..."

"I know exactly who and what Ivan Gold is." Patrick interrupted.

"Well sir, the others were pretty inconsequential." 7322 said extending his hand hoping Patrick would give the binder back to him without further investigation.

Patrick gave 7322 an inquiring look. "So, whom do you think you would pick from that selected group?"

"Sir, this binder is nonsense. Scribbled fantasies from a bunch of social misfits, sitting around, thinking and writing about end of the world scenarios. Sad really."

"Humor me." Patrick insisted.

"Well, Mr. President." 7322 continued, "if you were looking for a leader to manage a circumstance such as societal collapse and mass civil unrest, and I brought you three candidates; one a hunter, one a soldier and one a shepherd, who would you choose?"

Patrick thought for a moment. "The soldier or the hunter I guess." he replied.

"No," 7322 replied. "A soldier knows how to take orders. A soldier can be groomed to become a leader. Not all of them mind you. Turning a soldier into a leader takes time, organization and discipline. Three things G.R.A.SS does not possess."

"Ok, the hunter then." Patrick guessed.

"A hunter is an excellent choice for special operations. He works best alone or with a very small group on targeted operations. But not as a leader." 7322 responded. "To be prepared for the conflict ahead of us, we need a shepherd."

"How do you figure?" Patrick asked.

"This is a war on multiple fronts. One front is against the Skells. Another, against G.R.A.SS and the third against an increasingly anxious civilian population.

"What we need now is *control. Control* of physical movements of the infected. *Control* of communications to fight insurgency and *control* of the information given to the public.

"I'm not following you." Patrick said.

7322 continued. "The Shepherd knows how to herd his flock. How to manage a large group of individuals, and get them to move uniformly in the direction he wants them to go. And he knows how to steer them away from areas where he doesn't want them to tread.

"A Shepard knows how to eliminate any threat to his role, as the sole leader of the herd.

"The shepherd knows how to cut loose those within the flock that fall behind the rest and could slow the progress of the herd. While the shepherd desires a large herd, and wants to ensure all those he begins the day with are still there at the end of the day, he cannot show mercy to those that are weak.

Weakness from any member could jeopardize the lives and forward momentum of the entire herd.

"That is why we need a shepherd. Someone to guide these roving hordes of infected in the directions we want them to move. Whether that is towards containment zones, or into battle."

"You think these people, these...whatever they are, can be turned into soldiers?" The Commander in Chief asked.

"The infected can never be soldiers, but we need to stop thinking of them as just a liability. Right now, we see them as a threat that needs to be eliminated, but we need to change our tactics and turn them into assets," 7322 replied.

"I stopped those barbaric foaming chambers, now you want me to now weaponize the infected?" was Patrick's angry response.

"They are already weaponized, we just need to start considering how they are to be utilized. We have a state of martial law. The time may come when we need to reinstate the draft.

"The infected are still citizens, they can be conscripted into military service like everyone else." 7322 made this statement and then paused, waiting for the fierce push back from Patrick. It did not come.

7322 continued, "On the second front of this battle, we need someone who is going to capture the hearts and minds of those who support Ronan. They are not our not our enemies. They see Ronan not as a terrorist, but as the opposition party. This country has always had two party rule. That is until both parties literally consumed themselves.

"You are a President who was not elected but simply the last man standing.

"Ronan has exploited that and established himself as a political counterbalance, a check on your power, the opposing party. We know what he is, but others don't want to dig deep. His followers are those that fight against whatever is the current person or party in power.

"But to treat the followers of your political opponent with contempt and derision is to push them further into the other sides camp. It is counterproductive to keep attacking them and their leader. Trying to shame them into changing their allegiance is futile. You need to figure out what Ronan is saying to them that is resonating."

"And you think Colonel Tindall is that shepherd?" Patrick asked.

7322 nodded to the affirmative. "Look at him now. He is already leading a flock of lost sheep. Hiding out in the woods and suburbs. Moving place-to-place, keeping one step ahead of wolves and other predators. And by the way, we are one of the groups he and his followers perceive as their predators.

"Tindall is the man we need to lead. Now first we just need to get him to follow."

"Thank you for your insight 7322." Patrick said, closing and handing back the binder. "But this raid was your last action as leader of the Contractors." Patrick said.

"You were excellent in handing the press, 73...oh let's just drop the numbers crap, I am just going to call you Harry. Your days as a soldier are over, and it is time you became a statesman. You are going to continue to be the face of this administration as Harry Rose, Chief of Staff. Not 7322. I can't have you sitting in a suit and tie with the press during the day, and then leading commando team raids at night. We must have separation between Contractor activities and this administration."

"But sir, the entire state of New Jersey is basically operating as if it is a military internment camp, a forward operating base in hostile territory while dealing with the day to day activities any state deals with. The logistics that come into play for managing this situation, the recruiting of security forces, the managing of fleets of trucks that are rounding up Skells, the perimeter security..." Harry would have continued but was shut down by the Presidents raised palm.

"You need to have Daniel Sullivan handle these tactical matters moving forward. He has matured into a fine leader. He will take your place, and you will stay by my side." Patrick instructed.

Harry protested. "Thank you for your confidence, Mr. President, but still, these types of matters require professionalism, and 8105, or Daniel, is not ready to..."

He did not complete his sentence as Patrick slammed his hand down onto the desk, causing a glass of water to splatter onto his suit. Infuriated, the President picked up the glass and threw it across the room, where it shattered against the wall. He turned around and again faced a stunned Harry Rose.

"What the fuck did I just say!" Patrick yelled at Rose. "You need to learn the difference between when I am asking you for counsel, and when I am telling you the way it is! Do you know how many fucking people are trying to kill me right now? Do you!? Do you know the shit I am dealing with every day?! I am telling you I need you as my fucking full time Chief of Staff. Because that is what is needed of you right now!" Patrick screamed.

"Sir, I apologize" Harry said in a calming tone. "Of course, I am here for you, and I will ensure Daniel Sullivan is ready to handle any assignment."

CHAPTER 10:

Live from Trenton

Clifford Scott swirled the ice in his now empty glass to signal the bartender he was ready for another.

"Is that the guy from the news?" The attractive blond asked the bartender. She nodded to Clifford, who was too busy fussing with his hair in the mirror behind the top shelf of bottles to notice his admirer.

"Yep, that's him, he is here most every night before his live shot for the six o'clock. Probably won't be much longer, I hear he is getting a gig on the national news. Shame to lose him, as he is a good tipper and attracts a lot of pretty girls to this place. You are a good example." The bartender answered, his final flirtation going unnoticed by the blond, whose sights were already set.

She left her barstool and made her way over to her prey.

"So, where's your cameraman?" she asked the reporter.

Clifford turned around on his stool, annoyed at first, but upon observing the beauty of who was asking, he became fully vested in answering her any questions.

"Oh, I don't have one actually. I just set up the camera on the tripod and the feed goes live. Kind of a one-man show," he explained, his eyes taking in her fit body.

"I am so fascinated by the media, mind if I sit with you for a bit? You are the first celebrity I have ever met," she cooed.

Clifford looked at his watch. "Sure, but if you have time, why don't I show you the news van. I have thirty minutes before the live shot. In fact, how would you like to be on the air with me?"

"Stop, you're teasing me," she said, putting her hand on his chest and running her fingers down a couple of inches before resting her hand on his thigh.

"No seriously," he responded. "I am supposed to do one of those 'Man on the Street' interviews about how Trenton has declared itself a Skell sanctuary city. They tossed out all the Contractors and ceased rounding up of the infected. This saves me the time of having to grab people off the street. I can interview you. What do you say, would you like to be my interview subject?"

"I wouldn't know what to say," she giggled.

"Well, it is just a puff piece. How people are coping. How they go about with their daily lives with the Skells around. How they are happy that Trenton is a safe space for Skells now that the contractors are no longer allowed to operate here, etcetera."

She finished her drink and pushed away her glass.

"I really don't know much about those topics, but how about you show me the news van and you can fill me in." she purred.

Fifteen minutes later, Clifford emerged from the van, adjusted his tie and made sure his zipper was back up. He set up the tripod and unfurled the microphone chord. The blonde woman followed him outside the van, looking unconcerned about her tasseled hair and blouse. Clifford slid the door closed so the news channel logo was visible in the shot and gently positioned the woman so she was properly framed. He must have been good, he thought, as she seemed to still be on another planet. *Still got it.* He congratulated himself.

"OK, in a few minutes and you will see the light turn red on top of the camera," he explained.

"Hey!" he said and snapped his fingers in front of her face. "You still with me? When the light turns red, we will be live on the air. I will start off with some riffing about life among the zombies and such and then I am going to turn to you and ask how this crisis has affected your life. Ok?"

She said nothing, staring at him glassy eyed.

"I want you to look at the camera and not at me when you answer. Understood? Christ, I really put the spell on you, didn't I," he mumbled to himself, hoping that he would soon be getting higher quality trim once he hit the national network.

The two stood silently for a few more minutes, Clifford listening to the news desk banter in his earpiece waiting for the red light to come on. His interview subject was staring at him awkwardly. He gave her a sideways glance and wondered if she was high on drugs.

As the light turned on, so did Clifford.

"That's right guys," he said to the camera, referring to the two anchors that had just made his introduction. "I am out in front of a popular local gathering place to find out how people are coping."

"Clifford, it seems you have corralled some people to speak with." Clifford heard the anchorwoman say through his earpiece.

"Yes, that's right Olivia, I have asked one local Trenton resident I met to comment on the new sanctuary city law. Miss..."

As he turned to his interview subject, and was taken aback by how close she was now standing, her face mere inches from his own. She was no longer on the mark where he had asked her to stand. Her eyes now glazed, her mouth open, her breathing was more like panting.

"Umm..."

Was his last word before she lunged forward, digging her teeth into his throat and jerking her head backwards. The large piece of torn flesh had barely slid down her throat when she lunged again, her teeth tearing the skin from his right eye socket down to his jaw.

He heard screams coming from his ear piece, from around him and from his own mouth as he fell backwards, microphone still in hand, the attached chord pulled the camera down to the ground along with he and his attacker.

The blonde woman, framed in the live camera feed, began to rip open and devour the reporter's stomach.

CHAPTER 11:

Religion and Politics

D aniel walked into Harry Rose's office as he finished zipping up his fly and began struggling with the belt on his tactical PCRC uniform.

"Jesus fuck, your bathroom is hot. Like sauna hot. My balls were sweating like a whore in church in there!" Daniel brayed. Since childhood, he found foul language to be the spice that improved every conversation.

"Daniel..." Rose began to speak.

"And by the way," Daniel continued, ignoring his boss, "I just wrecked your toilet. I mean fucking wrecked it. You better give it a month to air out before you attempt re-entry."

"Daniel...." Rose again attempted to cut off his visitor's foul-mouthed rant.

Daniel was on a roll, laughing at his own vulgarity. "Or just condemn the fucking place to hell, I don't know if it is even usable again. I mean my precious pimpled ass just exploded..."

"Sullivan!" Rose yelled as Daniel finally stopped his monologue and looked up, only then noticing that there was a third party in the room.

"Mr. Sullivan," Rose continued, "this is Cardinal Remigio, he is here as an envoy from the Vatican. He is a special advisor to the church."

Cardinal Remigio corrected him. "I am a special advisor to the Holy See."

"Holy shit." Daniel said involuntarily.

The middle-aged man in the black suit and white collar turned around in his seat and looked disapprovingly at the crude Irishman. "Please, don't stop on my account, Mr. Sullivan," he said sarcastically as if he were addressing a naughty child. "Continue on with your account of your most recent visit to the commode."

Daniels Catholic school upbringing kicked in. He straightened his posture, rubbed his palm across his baldhead to straighten out hair that no longer existed and cleared his throat. "Hello Father. Cardinal?" he said sheepishly.

"Cardinal Remigio was telling us that the Vatican has grown increasingly concerned about the events of recent." Rose informed.

The Cardinal again turned to Harry Rose. "The Holy Father has dispatched me to determine if this is indeed a virus, or something more ancient, more biblical. If the latter, then the cure cannot be found in medicine, but in scripture. He feels that New Jersey is perhaps in need of an exorcism. And thus, he asked me for my professional evaluation and guidance."

Daniel let out an involuntary snort, and then realized that the man was serious.

"Cardinal Remigio is the Chief Vatican Exorcist. He is quite serious about this Mr. Sullivan." Rose chastised Daniel.

"Well Sir," Daniel said with as much humility as he could muster. "Please tell us anything we can do to assist with you while you are here. Um, and how long do you plan on being here?"

"I have a private jet at Newark. It will remain there until I can be sure that whatever is possessing this nation has been excised and I will then return to Rome where I will brief the Pontiff personally. These matters take time. In the meantime, I expect you will find me proper accommodations here."

"Absolutely Padre." Daniel said glibly, "There is an exceptional hotel about a mile from here that all the press is staying at. I will get you a room."

"I mean I expect accommodations here, in this building." Remigio explained.

"Well sir," Rose spoke up, "This facility is currently serving as the White House. The hotel is not far from here."

The Cardinal interjected again. "I believe this was a hotel before your occupation. I am sure you can find me a room here, there must be many available. I will need to be close to the President. Please feel free to ask him if you like. You will be informed that the Holy Father himself has called your President and has ensured my accommodation."

Daniel and Rose exchanged looks, neither wanted to approach President Patrick Callahan on this matter. "Of course." Rose said. "I will have one of my staff arrange a room for you. We will ensure you have proximity to the President."

"Thank you for your hospitality." Remigio replied. "Mr. Sullivan, there is another matter that I do believe you could assist me with. I understand you are also a man who has experience confronting demons."

"Excuse me?" Daniel replied.

"Demons in human form, I should've said. You have tracked down criminals. Warlords and other dangerous men who needed to be sought out and neutralized, haven't you?" Remigio asked, already knowing the answer.

"Well, I am more of a soldier who has performed specialized operations. I am not really a bounty hunter or mercenary. Not anymore." Daniel replied.

"From what I understand, you're not a solider anymore either, are you? From what I understand, you were dishonorably discharged from that duty. But I do have a special operation I need your assistance with, one that, if completed, would earn the appreciation of the church."

Daniel Sullivan gave a wary look over to Harry Rose, who returned a look that said, 'Just listen, keep your mouth shut and get this over with'.

The Cardinal continued. "We have received several disturbing threats against the Vatican. It seems that there is some deranged lost soul out there that is calling himself Pope Judas. We understand he has a small but fanatical group of followers, and they are making their way across the country towards New Jersey."

"Well, no issue there. Just let me know last known location and I will have a contractor team scoop them up. Problem solved." Daniel said confidently clapping his hands together.

"It's not that easy." Rose said, dampening Daniel's enthusiasm. "They have not committed any crimes that we know of or can prove. Right now, they are just a bunch of weirdos on a cross-country road trip. We can't pin any of the threats directly to them. We know who they are and as of an hour ago, where they were."

Rose turned his focus back to the Cardinal. "We were able to track them down through CCTV footage and vehicle license plate tracking systems. We pulled all their travel history since they left the west coast. We have had local authorities interview them, but so far, they have not so much as gone above the speed limit or blow through a toll."

"Can't we get him for misrepresentation or some shit... stuff" Daniel said correcting himself. "I mean like we would arrest someone for impersonating a cop?" he asked.

"On Halloween, a million people dress up as cops and walk around. It is not against the law unless you are trying to act like a cop. The guy can dress up and call himself Pope Judas, or Cardinal Crazy or Father Evil or anything else he wants to. This is still a relatively free, country." Rose said.

"The Pope, the true Pope, has called this man a spiritual disruptor, and he needs to be handled." Remigio said firmly.

Rose turned around his laptop to display a dashboard of video feeds. "See this Cardinal, this is Eye-Identify. We just deployed this new facial recognition technology state-wide. We simply add a photo or video of an individual to the database and we get immediately notified when that person is captured on camera. It can detect even non-compliant subjects. Glasses, fake beards or mustache, even plastic surgery won't fool our cameras. The system will automatically fill in the missing features. It works on an algorithm based on bone structure, dental structure and even the width between your eyes. People are like snowflakes, no two are identical."

The Cardinal seemed both pleased and disturbed by this technology.

"Don't worry sir," Rose said in a comforting tone. "I am putting my best men on this. We will keep an eye on this false prophet. If he enters New Jersey, we will know immediately."

Rose looked over at Daniel with a nod that signaled he was not going to give two seconds' worth of time or effort towards this nonsense, but wanted Sullivan to have his back nonetheless.

"Absolutely!" Daniel chimed in. "You can count on us Cardinal, you let the Vatican know there is only one Pope and we will ensure it remains that way." Daniel said, extending his hand to the Cardinal.

Remigio gave Daniel's hand a disgusted look, turned back to Rose, nodded, and walked out of the room without saying goodbye to either of them.

Rose collapsed back into his chair. "See the garbage I have to deal with," he said to Daniel in an annoyed tone. "I have the President starting to become as paranoid as Nixon, I have cyber terrorists who what to bring about end days, I have a press corps that are circling me like a school of sharks with blood in the water and I have you ranting about your toilet habits in front of holy men."

Daniel realized he was not helping the current situation, but he was not used to dealing with etiquette or working as part of a team, this was all new to the mercenary.

"Sorry 7322. I...I will work on my professionalism," he said, surprising even himself with such a tactful reply. Even Harry Rose raised an eyebrow impressed.

"Thank you, Daniel." Rose replied.

Daniel turned to leave the office.

"Oh, and Mr. Sullivan." Rose called after him, causing Daniel to stop and turn around.

"Moving forward, you can refer to me as Harry or Mr. Rose. As long as I am in this role, I am Harry Rose, not 7322."

"If you insist Harry." Daniel replied in a way that made 'Harry' sound like 'asshole'.

"And one more thing," Harry said. "Stay the fuck out of my shitter!"

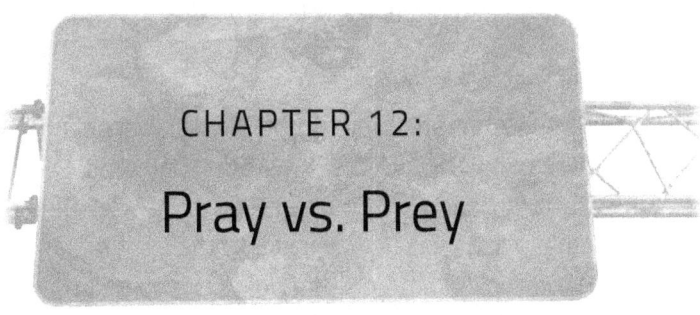

CHAPTER 12:

Pray vs. Prey

Harry Rose, was attempting to fit into his new, non-contractor, non-7322 persona. He had been requested to brief the President three times a day on ongoing operations and the status of the virus containment. The only person who was spending more time with the President than he was was Cardinal Remigio. The Cardinal had become a near constant presence at the side of the young President. While having no formal role in the administration, within days, he had his own room in the building, his own office, and unrestricted access to both the President's office and the President's ear.

Harry was relieved to see that the Cardinal was not present at this morning's briefing.

"We have been conducting a series of field tests on less than lethal counter-mobility agents to determine their effectiveness against the infected." Harry began. "The sonic and acoustic weaponry remains the most effective standard crowd control tools. Other tools like water cannons can be lethal to the more emaciated Skells. Standard items like tear gas and stench agents have had zero effect on them, especially when dealing with large gatherings of the infected. We had a couple of the DARPA egg-heads in here yesterday briefing us on Hunter-Prey relationships and swarming behavior to try and get a better understanding of how we can become more anticipatory than reactive on their migration patterns."

"Did the egg-heads confirm for you which is which?" Cardinal Remigio asked as he strolled into the briefing.

"Sir?" Harry replied not understanding the question.

"When discussing the non-infected versus infected relationship," the Cardinal continued, "which is the *hunter* and which is the *prey*?"

"Well sir, we each are both. It is a reciprocal hunter-prey relationship, they hunt us, and we hunt them. But we are not hunters out to kill our prey, merely contain. I cannot say the same for them." Rose answered.

"You used the term prey. I would use the term pray. Prayer is probably the most significant difference between us and these poor souls." Remigio added with a glance towards the President to ensure the commander was paying attention. "The difference between infected and uninfected is that only the uninfected can believe in and pray to god."

"Well there are considerable differences between the infected and those not exposed." Rose continued. "The infection significantly alters the..."

"Thank you, Mr. Rose that will be all," The President interrupted.

"Yes sir," Rose said chastened, realizing his relationship with the President was deteriorating by the day, and he did not know how to fix it.

Still stinging from the rebuke, he walked back to his office to find Daniel Sullivan sprawled out on the couch.

Rose walked over to his desk but did not sit down.

"How about you stand up when I enter. If you can't show respect for me, how about you show some respect for the fucking position I hold!" Rose snapped.

Daniel stood up, surprised by the harsh hello, but realizing that although he did not like the tone, he did appreciate the sentiment of the message.

Rose sat down himself, surprised that Sullivan complied to the barked order.

"Please, sit down. I didn't mean for that to come out as it did." he said in a much more civil intonation.

"Bad day at the office?" Sullivan asked while retaking his seat, hoping the jab would cool the tension in the room.

"Sorry Sullivan, I just got shown the door by the President. I was five minutes into my briefing. That Cardinal Remigio is getting into Callahan's head. The President is distancing himself from everyone. Perhaps Remigio is pulling him away."

"You aren't the only one around here to notice that, huh?" Daniel replied.

"Nope, and the President is addressing the nation tomorrow night, and I have not even seen his speech. No one has. He has been locked away with the Cardinal. This is bad. Polls are showing this Ronan character has a higher favorability rating than the President. And this guy is a murderous punk. You know how bad it is when you're polling lower than a sociopath?"

Rose opened his laptop and played the video stream of the Trenton reporter's last moments on camera. The video, less than a minute long, demonstrated how out of control the situation was. What bothered people most was not that the woman ripped out the reporter's stomach on live television. It was how normal the woman's physical appearance was before she did it. The public had also grown used to seeing emaciated Skells attacking, but VINNI's were a new paradigm.

"This has been viewed over six million times. Twenty-four hours after this was shot, Trenton had fallen. That was only a couple days after they kicked out your men. Our security teams are monitoring the CCTV feed from the city and could not find a single uninfected individual."

Sullivan shrugged.

"Jesus FUCKING Christ Sullivan, one of those things killed a news reporter live on the air! Do you know the fucking shit storm that has been come down on me from this!" Rose yelled while slamming his laptop shut.

He took a deep breath and calmed himself.

"So, you want to tell me what the hell happened in Trenton." Rose asked, no longer raging.

Sullivan knew this was going to be bad. "Look, I made a call and perhaps it was the wrong one. The Mayor there declared Trenton a sanctuary city. They demanded we stop the collection of Skells and even demanded that all contractors leave the city."

"And you did? You pulled your men out? The security teams, the collection teams?" Rose asked in disbelief.

"Sure, the Mayor was freaking out, so I figured we would pull back." Sullivan said, trying to justify his actions. "The city council had voted on it, and the mayor was really getting in my face. At the time, it seemed the most reasonable course of action. I figured, withdraw and let the mayor cool off a bit."

"Well he's cool alright," Rose retorted. "He's room temperature."

Sullivan shrugged again. "Well, I guess chalk this up as a learning opportunity for the rest of the state. That the contractors are there for their protection. Yet my guys have people on the street calling them fascists and spitting on them. Now they know our purpose."

Sullivan relaxed deeper into his chair. "No one really knows or appreciates what we do, until we stop doing it."

"Look, don't be so flippant about it. I have my hands filled here." Rose responded.

"Looks like we can bring Texas back into the fold but, now I have not only California claiming they want to secede but New Hampshire as well. Honestly, I could give a fuck about New Hampshire, but we need to end this crap with the west coast. No way are we losing that state on my watch."

Sullivan never had fondness for the left coast. "So, what can you do? Fuck em. How you gonna stop California from doing what they want to do?"

Rose threw his arms up in the air as if he were surrendering. "You know what, fuck it! You are right! We can plant a nuke on the San Andreas Fault line and another in the Cascadia Subduction Zone, that's what we can do. They want to secede; California can secede right into the fucking ocean! Los Angeles can change its name to Atlantis!"

Sullivan laughed.

"Sorry, now I am being flippant." Rose shook his head. "But you have got to lock this shit down Sullivan. We can't have mass carnage out there. At least we can't have it broadcast on live TV. Do you need more men?"

Sullivan was getting annoyed. "Look, stability operations are a process. This process takes steps. One step after the other. And each step takes time. If you told me you wanted a baby, I would tell you that to make a baby, I need one woman and nine months. Well, nine months and approximately thirteen minutes."

Harry Rose smiled.

Sullivan continued. "But that's the process and the time-line. One woman, nine months, bam, you got your baby. You can't shorten that timeframe to one month by giving me nine women. You aren't going to have your baby any sooner if I knock up nine women at the same time, trust me I've tried it."

Rose relaxed a bit. "I get it. But please, for now, do what you can, with what you have, in the time you have been given, ok?"

"Understood." Sullivan acknowledged. "Meanwhile I would appreciate if you could a handle on the media. I can't turn on the TV without some asshole calling the President a dictator and referring to my contractors as brown shirts and storm troopers." Sullivan requested.

"Trust me, it's on my short list." Rose replied.

"You know, I almost feel sorry for the real Nazi's out there." Sullivan pronounced.

"Excuse me?" A confused Rose queried.

"Think about it," Sullivan continued. "The Nazi's spent the last sixty years cultivating an image and building a brand. A brand that represents a small, yet very select, group of true sociopaths. Like you really, REALLY, had to work hard at becoming enough of a psycho, fucked-in-the-head outcast to be welcomed into the fold as a true Nazi. Now, all you have to do is put a Vote Callahan bumper sticker on your car and you are immediately called a Nazi. I mean, holy shit, talk about watering down the brand."

Rose was skeptical. "Are you repeating something you heard on the radio? One of your right-wing conspiracy shows?"

"No, I am serious, I realized this the other day." Sullivan continued and began mocking different voices.

"Hey, you don't believe mankind's farts are causing global warming? You're a Nazi. I mean, right now, it is tougher to get into community college than it is to get into the Nazis."

Rose chuckled. "You know Sullivan, when you put your mind to it, you can think some deep thoughts."

Sullivan accepted the compliment.

CHAPTER 13:

Antidote for Mortality

9104 walked into Harry Rose's office. She had a shit-eating grin on her face a mile wide. "We will soon have him! Pinksey is almost in our custody," she announced. "We can put him away for life just for the activities he was posting on the dark web."

"Dark Web?" Harry Rose asked

"It's like the internet, only for illicit activities. Criminals set up, for lack of a better description, storefronts. These could last an hour, a day or a week, but are usually only there for a brief period before taken down. Criminals sell everything from stolen identities, credit card numbers, and drugs and at its worst, human trafficking."

"As if the regular internet wasn't already a fertile breeding ground for deviancy," he commented.

"Well, Pinskey had taken even the Dark Web to new levels of depravity."

"So, what's Pinskey in to?" He could tell by her hesitation and the look on her face that it was bad. "Go ahead." he urged, "I have not had lunch yet, may as well go ahead and kill my appetite."

She exhaled, "Seems Pinskey was offering the cure for death, the antidote for mortality as he puts it. He was offering VINNI's for rich dying people to have sex with. He had been telling them that by bedding a VINNI, they would become one themselves, kind of like inoculating themselves from all sorts of future disease, while curing them of their current issues."

"So, he is a pimp. A virus pimp, but a pimp nonetheless. He'll post bail and be gone." Harry said dismissively.

"There is much more to his offering. Right now, only a handful of us here know about this, but if this gets out, there could be copycats. Other sick bastards who would..." She faded off.

"Ok, so seems like you buried the lead. Why don't you give me the full picture?" he said, giving her his full attention.

"These were not willing men and women that Pinskey was pimping out. He had been identifying them in the public. Tracking their whereabouts. He builds profiles on them and allows the wealthy clients to choose which one they want. When they choose, Pinskey's men go out and kidnap the person, restrain them and force them into sex slavery."

"Jesus."

"It's gets worse."

"How? How could it be worse than that?" an incredulous Harry Rose replied.

"Once the client finishes having sex with the VINNI, the client then goes through the transformation caused by exposure to the virus. If they are fat, they become thin. If they are dying, they become well. But either way, even with no outward sign of infection, they are still carriers of the virus. There were other postings from people who have been involved in activity. They warn that not all the clients survive the process."

"The virus kills them?" Harry asked.

"We have heard multiple stories. Some die because the VINNI was not properly restrained and devours their partner after sex. Some cannot handle the post sex infection. The transformation the person goes through after having sex with a VINNI. It...it's pretty brutal. Think of the worst case of food poisoning imaginable, and then multiply that by ten."

"I get the picture." Harry held up his hand, as he did not need further explanation.

"Once the client is satisfied with the transformation, the VINNI can't just be released. The sexual act sets off a change that turns the VINNI psychotic. They exhibit the same symptoms we associated with standard Skell virus, extreme violence, mutilation and cannibalism of the client or whomever they had sex with. This state can't be reversed until the VINNI is fed human flesh. So, this creates a couple of options for Pinskey and his clientele.

"He can feed the VINNI human flesh, which will turn them back into their normal state, and then hold them to be raped again and again. This is not particularly easy, as you can just run down to the corner store and pick up a pound of flesh. So, someone has to be murdered to keep a VINNI in working order."

"I feel like there is going to be some sort of obscene 'OR' coming." Harry said while rubbing his eyes with his thumb and forefinger.

"Or," 9104 continued confirming his suspicion. "For a few dollars more, the client can choose to hunt their own VINNI."

"You're fucking kidding me?" Harry said incredulously.

"Nope, wish I were. He calls it an underground fuck-n-hunt club. If the client shells out a cool million dollars, Pinskey will arrange for the john to track and hunt down the chosen VINNI after sex. Kind of like going to the restaurant and picking a lobster from the tank that you want to eat for dinner. That is, if you were having sex with the lobster in-between choosing it and eating it."

Harry sat stunned for a moment. "Ok, I see why this needs to be kept quiet. We want these people, these VINNI's, to come out of the shadows, to not fear the government is going to do something bad to them just because of their circumstance, and it turns out they indeed do have a lot to fear."

"We found his location and we have it surrounded. Due to the circumstances, I don't want this to be handled by local authorities. Word will spread out afterwards about what they found in there. I need your permission to take the facility that Pinskey and his men are holed up in. I need you to ok use deadly force if necessary."

Rose was hesitant to have her face Pinskey and his men again. The last time the met, she was left bloody on the ground by Pinskey's hand and Rose could do nothing but stand, held at gunpoint, and watch.

"I am coming with you," he volunteered.

"Sir, this is no longer your role. You are not wearing the uniform anymore. We will take Sullivan, I mean 8150."

Rose felt something he did not like to feel. A slight pang of jealousy. Instead of kicking doors and asses he was the third wheel between the President and the Cardinal.

"Ok," he said. But before he could issue a further warning, two contractors came into the room.

One man handed her an iPad. She flipped through the pictures, and then opened an application that displayed a live feed video. Rose noticed that whatever she was looking at, it was getting her pissed.

"Is this real time, is this happing now?" she snapped. "I told them not to move in until I arrived! What the hell happened?"

The man began to quietly whisper to 9104 but she shot him down. "Quit the pillow talk, this whole mission has gone tits up, you may as well tell us all what went wrong."

The contractor cleared his throat. "Well, sir, ma'am. We were watching the grounds that Pinskey was holding the, um, prisoners and we were keeping an eye on them and waiting for you when a dozen guys showed up and walked right up to the door. We thought it was some sort of bachelor party or something, a bunch of guys going to have sex with the girls inside. But these guys did not look right."

"How many did you say there were?" Rose asked.

"We counted thirteen, but only twelve entered the building. It happened so fast. The group went up to the front door, kicked it open and poured in. We did not know what to do, till we heard screams and all sorts of ruckus going on in there. Soon as we heard the first shots ring out, we moved in."

"Well, what did you find, who were these guys?"

The contractor continued. "These guys were beating the shit out of Pinskey's men. They freed the hostages and were just going around wrecking the place and beating on whomever put up a fight."

"Were they heavily armed?" Rose asked.

"That's' the weird part. Not a weapon among them, other than some walking sticks, their fists and sandals."

"Sandals?" she asked.

"Yeah, some had them taken their sandals off and were using them to smack the shit out of Pinskey's goons. They were holding their own until Pinskey's guys pulled out guns and started shooting them. We raced in and put an end to it. Pinskey got away through a window. But we smashed his operation and we rescued over fifteen infected men and women. "Christ almighty, we can't have groups of vigilantes running around trying to do our jobs. Who is this group, and why did they go in?"

"Silent as the snow, sir," he replied. "Not one has said a word."

"They are waiting for lawyers most likely." 8150 sneered.

"No ma'am" he replied. "They just won't speak. They are all together in one room, but silent as the crypt. Not a word at all, it's creepy. No asking for a lawyer, no mouthing off as we hauled them in. They came peacefully. They have no ID's on them, no wallets, no nothing. We offered them lawyers but they won't talk to them either."

"They must have some sort of ID, a phone on them, or driver's license?" she asked.

"Nothing, only thing each one had on his person was a pack of playing cards."

"What do you mean, like they were sitting around and playing go fish?"

"No sir, these are not your dollar store cards. These are casino quality poker cards. I have been to Atlantic City enough to know the real thing, although these cards didn't come from Atlantic City casino, these cards all came from some casino in Las Vegas.

"My first thought was that these guys came here looking for an illegal poker game and when they found out they were in the wrong spot; they began busting up the join. But the pieces don't fit together. They seemed to be more focused on wrecking the place than even rescuing the VINNI's. They were there for Pinskey only, and did not put up a fight against our people.

"One more thing. Each deck of cards had a single hold drilled through the center. Like someone drove a nail through the deck. Like when casino's drill holes through a deck when they throw one out, so cons can't use them to rig games. But this somehow seemed like more than that, like it meant something to these whack jobs. Twelve guys each with a single deck of cards, each with a hole drilled through the center of the pack."

"Well, sweat it out of them, one of the thirteen will crack eventually." Rose offered.

"Um, eleven sir. During the initial raid and confusion, one of the twelve escaped and he and the guy who waited outside vanished. I had a ton of back up outside, but none of them saw the getaway. It was like the two were there, and then they were gone."

"He won't get far." Rose said calmly. "He is forced out into the open now. And in the open is where it gets easy to find him," he said cryptically.

CHAPTER 14:

The Camp: Part I

James and Fiona Sullivan had been duped into pulling their car over on the highway to help what they thought was a motorist in distress. The set up was meant to just steal their car and not to harm them. But the two were recognized by their would-be carjackers. Once identified as having close ties to the current administration, they became more valuable than their car. They were detained and politely escorted by Colonel Tindal and Jack "Smoothie" Jones to a clearing in the woods that had been turned into a hidden campground. Tents and temporary structures had been established, and what appeared to be more than two hundred people milled about in the secret encampment. Most appeared to be civilians, men and women, young and old. There was a small group of heavily armed military personnel protecting the camp, but most of the residents were unarmed. James and Fiona could not imagine who these people were, why they were hiding, whom they were hiding from and why they had such interest in detaining the two of them. These people certainly did not appear to be being held against their will. James observed that the men with guns were in a protective stance.

Children were playing in front of a large tent that appeared to be cafeteria. Medical student Fiona instinctively scanned the area for what would serve as an infirmary.

The atmosphere seemed casual and confident, not fearful, not intimidating. Almost welcoming.

"Hey cancer boy," said a female voice directed at James.

"What?" James turned around and looked flustered at the thin, attractive blond woman. She was in her twenties but dressed like a high school kid, with ripped jeans and tee shirt that did not hide her midriff.

"You, the dead man walking," she said again.

Jim did not respond but continued to stare at her trying to figure out who she was and how she knew him. He had not told anyone about his diagnosis. If she worked for his oncologist, she sure had some piss poor ideas of patient confidentiality.

"What is she talking about?" Fiona asked looking at James.

"Nothing. She's obviously off her meds. Ignore her." James said calmingly to Fiona.

James and Fiona continued following Colonel Tindall into one of the only fully constructed cabins that was serving as his office and residence. The three of them sat down in a series of faux leather chairs that were positioned in a semi-circle next to a white board on the wall.

"I call this area the Pitt. This is where we welcome new comers and discuss strategy." Tindall informed them, as the heavy-set man from the road who had initially flagged them down walked in carrying a cooler. "This is my right-hand man, Mr. Jones."

"Jack," Jack said to them. "My apologies for the ruse on the highway, but we were never going to harm you. We just needed your vehicle." The heavyset man held out a portable cooler. "Here, I brought you some cold drinks, I have both soda and, if you like, there are some adult beverages in there as well."

Jack grabbed a diet soda and fell heavily into one of the seats.

"You see," Tindall continued, "we were going on the assumption that our time here was running out. We were simply too many. We needed to be prepared for quick mobility and thus, we needed as many vehicles as possible. But who would have known that the answer to our problem would come to us inside one of those cars."

Fiona and James exchanged looks. James tensed up, he looked around and figured he could fight his way out of the room, but he was unsure how he could do so while also protecting Fiona. The Colonel noticed James subtle change in posture was that of a man preparing for battle.

"I don't want you to be concerned." Tindall said calmingly. "We simply have an opportunity for you. An opportunity to save many lives and prevent violence. These people here, they are not my prisoners, they sought me and my men out, for protection. These people have been re-born by this virus. Some were bitten, some ate the tainted food supply, and some followed directions they read online for rapid weight loss. These are the lucky ones, the people who have fallen victim to this plague and survived."

"I had seen postings about this." Fiona chimed in. "Very heavy people seem to be able to burn the virus out before it takes full control of them. I thought it was bullshit." James shot her a disapproving look, he did not like to hear his baby sister talk like that.

"It's all true." Tindall replied. "Now, these people are being sought out. We hear contractors are rounding them up along with the Skells, Taking them somewhere. To be turned into super soldiers is my guess. They would make superior weapons. They don't seem to need food, not the type we eat anyway. They are physically healthy, in fact most are much healthier than they were before the virus."

James looked over at Jack Jones, who had a diet soda in one hand and a jelly donut in the other.

"What about you Jack?" James commented. "You seek out the Colonel?"

Jack chuckled. "Do I look like I am too concerned about my weight? I sought out the Colonels help and guidance for other reasons. Not everyone is obsessed with their outward appearance. The Colonel has been an immense help to me on the inside."

"And now it is my time to help these people one final time." Tindall said. "And that is why you are here. I don't want this president's private army of contractors coming in here and trying to take this camp by force. It is only a matter of time before we are discovered. I am not looking for a shootout with the contractors and not looking for these people to be harmed or turned into lab rats to be studied or imprisoned. I want you to go back to the President. Jack will accompany you. Tell him I will turn myself in and face whatever punishment is waiting for me for what happened back at FOB Prince. In exchange, I would like to ensure my men who served under me and then, accompanied me when I went AWOL, face no charges. They were soldiers and they were following their commanding officer. Nothing more. Will you do that for me?"

James and Fiona both nodded in agreement.

"Thank you." The Colonel said, relieved his command was finally coming to a peaceful end. "Now Jack will take you to get something to eat before the drive back."

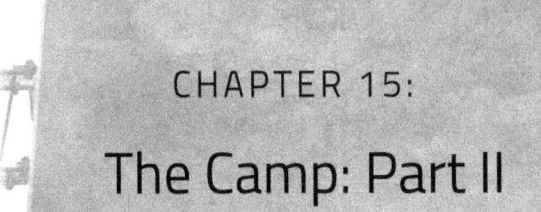

CHAPTER 15:

The Camp: Part II

"Hello again cancer boy," said a familiar voice.

Fiona and James ignored the strange shout out and continued following Jack through the camp towards the kitchen.

"Yeah, you, I know you can hear me," she repeated her taunt. She was thin and beautiful. Standing with her hands on her hips in a cocky fashion.

James and Fiona turned around and faced Bethany.

"So, who's your friend?" she asked, hinting to find out what the relationship was between him and Fiona.

"That is my little sister. She is a medical student." James answered, not quite sure why.

"You the new camp doctor?" Bethany asked.

"No." Fiona replied. "We were brought here; they took our car. But to be honest, I am kind of glad they did. This place is fascinating. I really want to talk to some of these people, if possible examine them, especially the..." she was at a loss for description.

"VINNI's." she replied. "That is the politically correct term. Virus Infected, Non-Necrotic Individuals. It means we did not turn into one of those brainless zombies. Well, I should not call them brainless. They actually have two brains now."

"Oh, that's public knowledge now?" Sullivan realized. "No need to deny it. An unfortunate side effect of prolonged exposure to the infection. Two brains, but no mind."

"They have two brains?" Fiona asked.

Sullivan responded, forgoing any precept of not sharing confidential information. "They can't think and reason like we do, but they still possess a mind, one that can handle baser instincts, hunt, kill, and eat. Hopefully they can't fuck. I have seen some ugly kids in my day, but I can't imagine what that offspring would look like."

"Wait, so when you are saying the infected have two brains? Is that like a euphemism, like when you say a guy is thinking with his little head and not his big head?"

No one responded to Fiona's inquiry.

James slapped his hands together with a loud clap. "Well it has been fun catching up," he said sarcastically. "But if you will excuse me, we are going to grab a bit to eat and be on our way. Mr. Jack Jones here is going to escort us back home."

"The kitchen tent is just over there." Jack pointed.

The woman turned to Fiona "Honey why don't you and Jack go grab some food and save us a table, I want to talk to your big bro for a little bit, ok?"

Fiona gave James a look, and he nodded that it he would be fine. She walked off with Jack towards a large tent in the center of camp.

"How is the food here?" James asked.

"I wouldn't know I have not been hungry for days."

James glared at her, but did not respond. He searched her face for some sort of recognition. Was she from his doctor's office? Perhaps the pharmacy? She was too attractive for him to have forgotten meeting her.

"Who are you?" James asked.

"No one you know, or have met before. I don't know you either," she replied, her casual, perky attitude did not reflect the morbid way she began the conversation.

"How could you tell, tell that I was...?" James asked.

"Was a dead man walking?" she said, continuing to needle James. "It's the cancer. I could smell it on you, like you stepped in dog shit," she replied, her smile not wavering.

"Hey fuck you!" he replied to the insensitive bitch.

"You're going to die you know," she said, telling him something he already knew.

"Thank you for that, just what I needed to hear," he replied and started walking away.

"You don't have to," she called after him. "Die that is."

He ignored her and kept walking. "I said you don't have to, that is if you don't want to. But trust me, if you want to die, there are quicker ways to do it than the way you're going about it now. Ways that are quicker and less agonizing then letting that cancer eat away at you."

James turned around and moved towards her at a quick threatening pace to which she showed little concern. "Look I don't know if you are some kind of doctor or health guru or whatever, but I have seen the best and there is no cure for me."

"There was no cure, there is one now." She continued her cryptic bullshit.

"What are you some sort of vitamin salesman?" James snapped.

"No, not a doctor, not a faith healer, not a salesman. I am, or was, a computer nerd to be exact. But I was dying, just like you. And I had given up hope, just like you. I had high blood pressure, high cholesterol, early stage heart disease, and a body mass of, well, let's just say, when I sat around the house."

"Yeah, well all that shit is reversible. My cancer was not brought on by bad lifestyle choices. You going to give me some shit that you discovered hot yoga and it cured your ills? What I got isn't reversible, and it isn't curable. I can't just drop some weight and take a pill. My problem is my cells, not cellulite." James snapped.

"You haven't heard of what's going on, have you? Let me guess, not an online chat room kind of guy. I can tell, you are a doer. You've lived your life in the real world, not cyber." She flirted, eyeing him up and down. "This virus, there are ways to manage the transmission. It's not for everyone who is sick, but if the recipient can handle it...well, you look like a guy that can handle himself." She caught herself. 'Christ,' she thought, what the hell is wrong with her, she needed to pull her libido back into check.

"Go on." James prodded intrigued.

"There are ways to get just enough exposure to the virus to gain all the benefits of infection, without it killing you. Kind of like chemotherapy or radiation. The right dose, your cured. Receive a bad dosage, you take a dirt nap." she explained.

"And what, you have some sort of transfusion area here?" James asked.

"Well," Beth shrugged, "kind of, but unlike chemo, the transfusion process is a lot more pleasant."

"Look," James said, getting annoyed. "I understand you're one of those people who survived the virus, but like I said..."

"I did not say you were going to be cured by getting thin," she interrupted him. "Well, you will get thinner, but you are not going to drop a metric ton like I did. But it will still cure you. This virus, it is not just a curse. To a few, it is a cure. It is the miracle we have all been waiting for. You just have to know how to administer it."

"Yeah, and you know how huh? You possess this fucking knowledge." James snapped.

"Funny that you call it 'fucking knowledge', as that is not too far off," she said with a sly smile. "Tell you what, let's go for a little drive. Tell your sister to head on without you. She will be safe with Jack. You give me one night, and I will give you your life back."

CHAPTER 16:

WTF Are Acronyms

BMW and Sullivan walked down the corridor on their way to the morning security briefing with the President. Sullivan was hurting from the night before, a rare night outside the compound where the only thing he was killing was his brain cells.

BMW looked over at his hung-over partner. "Sullivan, you need to grow up. Think of your future, think about starting a family."

Sullivan looked back with bloodshot eyes. "Says the man whose only human relationship seems to be with me."

"That is because we are in a state of emergency right now. Once this entire zombie shit is over, I am out of here. I am going to get my own helicopter start my own business and start my family."

Sullivan smiled. "OK, so give me some advice love doctor. How do I go about starting this domesticated future you think is so great?"

BMW smirked "For one thing, stop dating strippers."

Sullivan balked. "I love strippers. There are so many added benefits. For instance, every time you go down on one, you come up with a dollar bill stuck between your teeth."

"Man, that's nasty." BMW replied. "Also, you need to start stepping up. Rose is going to be top dog and you seem to be his choice for second in command. You need to begin strategizing a plan."

Sullivan again balked. "I don't do strategy. I leave that up to the big thinkers. I am a tactical guy. I am the guy who enforces the strategy without thinking. The fifty-pound brains, they are the ones that think shit up and develop strategy. As long as there are zombies, I am keeping my brain as small as possible."

The two men entered the conference room and got the glare from those who had arrived on time. They found two seats next to each other at the back of the room. Across the room, he saw Rose huddled with 9104.

"What do you think is up with those two?" BMW asked, his curiosity more focused on the attractive 9104 than their boss.

"I know what you are thinking" Sullivan warned. "And I would set your sights on another woman to find your domestic goddess. I don't know what the history is between them, but I would not get in the middle. Plenty of fish out there, don't hunt in the big dog's territory."

As the President entered the briefing room, the rest of the attendees stood at attention. Usually the President would enter alone, or with his scheduling assistant. Now he was rarely without the company and council of Cardinal Remigio.

Mr. Spencer began the briefing with an announcement that several innovative programs will be launched to bring the Skell menace under control.

Daniel Sullivan and BMW entered the room as Spencer was beginning to speak getting a disapproving look from President Callahan.

"We are making great strides in establishing agencies, programs and reporting procedures too.

"I know you have been very concerned you were not receiving all the pertinent data you needed Mr. President, so starting tomorrow, each morning you will receive a report keeping track on all new cases, the rate of our containment teams rounding up those new cases and any unfortunate virus caused loss of life in the Daily Infected, Contained, Killed report."

BMW leaned over and whispered in Sullivan's ear "Otherwise known as the DICK report."

"We have deployed drones in our new Aerial Skell Surveillance program."

"Otherwise known as ASS program." BMW again murmured under his breath.

"Also, a new division has been stood up, which can be quickly assembled and dropped into unstable areas. We are calling these elite units Tactical Insertion Teams."

"TITS." BMW whispered to Daniel.

"Excuse me, Mr. Spencer," Sullivan said while raising his hand like he was in second grade. "But aren't there a couple of those units already firmed up?"

"Yes, there are." Spencer responded.

"I thought so, they work most effectively in pairs." Sullivan replied.

Spencer looked at Sullivan confused. "Um, ok."

"Mr. Spencer," Sullivan asked, again raising his hand, "would it be possible to have myself and Mr. White, embedded into a pair of Tactical Insertion Teams?"

Spencer gave a self-satisfied grin, as he had never received such interest from the contractors. "I am sure that can be arranged, glad you are on board Mr. Sullivan. Mr. White."

Sullivan gave a wink to BMW.

Harry Rose had already caught onto the game. "Please refer to Mr. Daniel Sullivan as 8150 and Mr. Malcolm White as 8080." Rose needed to ensure they understood the organizational structure, and where Sullivan and White fell in the pecking order.

A chastened Mr. Spencer continued. "Of course, Mr. Rose. To continue, we have begun deploying new civilian led Domestic Operations Policing Enterprise, which will allow citizens to patrol their own neighborhoods and of course, report cases of infection, as well as citizens that are being non-compliant to the new curfew and regulations."

"What was the name of that program again?" BMW asked.

"Domestic Operations Policing Enterprise." Spencer responded

"DOPE." BMW said.

Spencer smiled. "Thank you, I think it's pretty cool or 'dope' as well." Spencer was glowing with the approval he was receiving.

"May I ask, what your new role is within these organizations?" VP Rose asked.

"Yes sir, my official title is the head of the overarching integration center to ensure all the programs and the systems work together cohesively," he replied considerably puffed up. "My official title is Director Integration Command, Systems Unification Center."

"DIC SUC?" Sullivan said, finally getting the gist of the game.

BMW turned to Sullivan "Don't these names need to go through a marketing department or some such shit?"

Spencer then picked up the remote control and clicked on the large television monitor on the wall.

"One of our new Unmanned Arial Systems programs is being featured on the morning news right now."

The newscaster was finishing his prior story. "The man was arrested for holding two women captives as sex slaves. Police found him and his victim's location when they replied to an advertisement the suspect had posted on an underground web portal used for human trafficking. A truly disturbing story. Next up, the Infection Containment Teams are rolling out a new program to help safely assemble groups of infected while keeping themselves and the public safe."

The television news program switched to live video being streamed from the news copter flying above a Jersey suburb.

"That's right Roger," the helicopter reporter began. Unmanned Aerial Systems, or more commonly called drones, are being employed to control the infected. We have our own manned aerial helicopter monitoring the demonstration from a safe distance. This town has become overpopulated with roaming infected, the administration's new Robotic Arial Police Enforcement teams or RAPE teams. Wait, is that correct?" The reporter asked, flipping through the papers on his desk. "Well that is a name that was not thought through."

A slap could be heard in the room as BMW's palm met his forehead.

The reporter continued. "As you can see the two contractors there are viewing the drone footage on an iPad. We can see, three blocks away, the movement of a large crowd of infected. They seem to be moving in the direction of the contractors, so I am sure the contractors will use the drone to migrate them away. Umm, they seem to be getting pretty close, almost too close for comfort I would say."

The video displayed a large horde of infected following the drone through the streets, only one block away from where the two contractors stood. The two men could be seen staring intently at a tablet, which was displaying for them the live stream video from the drone. They seemed oblivious to the proximity of drone and the Skells to their own location.

"The contractors seem to be fixated on the video stream from the drone camera and are not paying attention to their surroundings." The reporter stated, his cracking voice revealing his growing concern.

"Good lord, the crowd is moving directly towards them. Does anyone have their cell phone numbers or...?" The reporter's cadence was no longer that of a smooth television news reporter but one of a man about to witness horror with no way to prevent it.

"My god! Look up! Look up from the screen you idiots!" The reporter yelled, as if the two men could hear him over the blades of the copter.

"Oh, Jesus Christ, cut away, cut away!" The man shrieked as the two oblivious contractors were seen on camera looking up from their drone view only in time to see the hands and teeth of three dozen Skells that descended upon them, ripping them to bloody shreds on live TV.

"Ladies and gentlemen, I am sorry you had to see that." The newsroom anchorman said somberly to the camera. "Obviously, this is a program that needs to be more thought out. We are going take a commercial break as our thoughts and prayers go out to those two men and their families."

Rose stood and turned off the television with a remote. "Spenser," he began, "could you please conduct some research to try and gage just how many fucking people need to be eaten on live TV before the public begins to lose confidence in the administration's ability to handle this crisis!"

Spenser stood and begun to write himself a note in his small notebook, until he felt the remote shattering as it struck the side of his head.

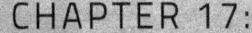

CHAPTER 17:

The Camp: Part III

Bethany led James into her tent. It was well equipped, filled with newly purchased, top of the line camping equipment. It had all the amenities one could purchase at an upscale sporting goods store, for those that want to go camping, yet not rough it or even be remotely uncomfortable.

She sat down on the bed in a seductive manor, while James remained just inside the entrance.

"Zip the door closed please." she requested.

He felt awkward, but complied with her request.

"Try not to run out of the tent screaming like a little bitch from what I am going to tell you, I can see you are nervous," she said with continued ball busting attitude.

James became self-conscious, realizing his apprehension and confusion were radiating like rosacea. He manned up and walked over to the folding chair across from her and awkwardly positioned his bulky frame into the small chair of canvas and aluminum.

"Just tell me what you have to tell me," he replied.

"Ok, first off, full disclosure. I was infected after a one-night stand." She paused to await his response, of which there was none, so she continued. "Have you heard about the transmission of the virus to people who become VINNI's or Virus Infected Non-Necrotic Individuals? How some people have been seeking it out, and the immediate after effects? I mean, people have been posting all sorts of tales on the web."

"I have been a little pre-occupied as of late." James responded, being one of the rare individuals with no web presence, no Facebook, no Snapchat, not even a personal email address. A man, who, other than checking sports scores, had no interest or reason to go online.

"Just over a week ago, I was morbidly obese," she explained. "I got infected from a steak I ate for dinner. I went through all the hell that all infected go through soon after exposure. I will save you the disgusting details. But then, when the night of horror and symptoms that caused my transformation were over, I was the new me. I became what you see before you," she said with a wave of her hands to draw attention to her figure. "I have absolutely no desire to eat your flesh, though I have to admit, you are yummy. But I would have thought of you as yummy prior to my infection," she flirted.

"So once the virus burned out, is it dead, are you, are you virus free now?" James asked.

"No, not at all," she said sadly. "The virus is still very much alive inside me, but not enough to continue its damaging effects. But I am contagious. So, that is why I wanted to warn you. I am talking about transmitting the infection to you. You will then be infected. Forever. Or at least until they find some sort of cure."

"OK, I am assuming people like you, VINNI's, will be contagious for life. Kind of like herpes. I can see a whole new line of dating apps appearing." James said, trying to lighten the mood.

"I was a software developer; well I guess I still am. And yes, I have already began coding a dating app, for people, as you say, like me. Perhaps I will be the next billionaire."

"Well what does this have to do with me?" James asked

"Well, look, I don't know how to put this delicately, but you know you don't have much time left, you do know that correct? I mean, I don't know how I can tell, but I can. I hoped I was not giving you a diagnosis you were not aware of." She leaned forward while talking and put both her hands on his knees.

"I am all too aware of my condition and its progression." James resigned.

"Well, now there is another option. You could be come, as you say, like me," she said gently.

"Infected? You will infect me and make me a VINNI?" he replied, ensuring he was following.

"You make it sound so romantic," she said, sitting back in her chair.

"Sorry, I did not mean that to come out that way. Look, you are trying to help me, I understand that, I appreciate that, I am just confused."

"How long have they given you?" she asked.

"Weeks. Months optimistically. But I have chosen not to undergo the treatment route, not going to spend my last days on this earth being pumped with poison and sick as a dog."

"I believe, if things go correctly, you could spend less than twenty-four hours sick as a dog, and come out of it cancer free. And I think I can offer that to you. I have not done this before. The reason I chose you is that I am not 100 percent sure this would work. If you just had something manageable, like diabetes, I would not suggest this. But I could tell you did not have much time left. So, what have you got to lose?"

"If I were to become like you, infected, or a VINNI, what is the downside? Why wouldn't everyone want to take this cure?" James questioned.

"Well, you know when you watch those drug ads on TV and after they say all the benefits of the drug, they spend the second part showing beautiful images and happy people, meanwhile a voiceover tells you of all the possible horrible gross side effects?" she asked

"Yeah, if your erection lasts more than four hours, etcetera." he confirmed.

"Exactly, and I must say, it's both ironic and fitting that you chose that particular prescription drug advertisement. Now let me tell you about the possible side effects of my treatment."

CHAPTER 18:

The Camp: Part IV

Bethany continued. "Ever since I transformed, I have gone through phases where I have been as horny as a sailor back from sea. It is almost overwhelming when the urges come over me. Christ, listen to me, I am even talking in sexual innuendo."

James chuckled at the double entendre.

"At first I thought it was this new body," she said, standing up and giving a brief twirl to show off her body as if it were a new dress she had just put on. "The way men suddenly noticed me, paid attention to me, and not in the usual 'point and make fat jokes' way.

"I thought it was just the fact that I could suddenly have any man I wanting that made me so aroused. Then I realized that the feelings I was experiencing were almost uncontrollable. You have no idea how intense and blinding the urges can be."

James cleared his throat. "Excuse me, I was once a sixteen-year-old boy once..." James winked and trailed off.

She smiled, but only for a brief second, as the memories returned to her.

"The feelings. They were not passion, but possession." she continued.

"I can only imagine they are like what a heroin or crack addict goes through. Well I succumbed to that urge, found a guy and I took him home to rid myself of this craving. After we finished. Well, I should say, after HE finished, the darker side of the cure kicked in.

"There were no little booklets on the pill jar or fast talking commercial spokesman to tell me what the big, whopping, four-hour-erection, type side effect was of the cure I had been given.

"I don't recall exactly how it happened, but immediately following intercourse, I killed and ate the poor man I'd brought home."

She kept her eyes focused on the floor, afraid to look up and see whatever expression would be on James's face. She waited to see if he would get up and leave, or call her out for being the murderous cannibal she knew she was, or to exact revenge on her for his fellow fallen dude. He did none of the above.

She looked up at him. "Did you understand what I just said, I was not exaggerating. I killed the man and I ate him, right there, in the very bed we'd just shared."

"Go on." James said emotionless.

"Well, ok, that was the kind of the big reveal to the story here. I did not want to sugarcoat it for you. I have not had sex since." Beth embarrassedly confessed.

"Look," James said. "I am not a cop, or a shrink. I am not even a contractor anymore, and I am no moral judge. This is a troubled time, and people have done terrible things. I am not going to tell anyone. I understand, that if I get this cure from you, I too will have these urges. I could go all Hannibal Lecter. Is that what you are warning me about?"

"Yes," she replied

"Well, I think a life of celibacy is still better than death," he said.

"So, you want to continue our talk? Because what I am going to suggest gets a little weird," she said coyly.

"I am all ears," he replied.

"I think, that we can help each other." she continued. "I want to see what would happen if I were restrained. If we went somewhere, a hotel room, and you tied me up. I am not talking *Fifty Shades* here with fuzzy handcuffs and Velcro. I am talking real restraints, where you fully secured me to the bed."

"Hey, whatever floats your boat." he joked.

"I am serious. If you secured me, and then we did it. You know, had sex. I think it would provide you with enough exposure to the virus to turn you like me. But also, I want to see how long the post sex, kill and eat urges, would last.

"Will the feelings go away after an hour or two? And, if you yourself turn, and you become like me, would I still feel those urges to kill you or do these urges only force us to kill the uninfected." she paused. "Christ almighty, just listening to what I am saying is a mind fuck. I feel like I am losing it."

"No, you are not. And yes, these are good questions. I want to explore this with you." James said his confidence fully restored.

"You are sure? There is no going back." she warned.

"I have nothing to go back to. I need to talk to my sister. I am not going to share with her everything that we discussed. I want to be able to say good-bye if this does not work. I will tell her you are an old girlfriend, one I did not recognize at first, but one I want to re-connect with."

Bethany felt relieved. "That is a good cover story, and I want to be fully honest with you, I am not doing this just for you. This is not purely an altruistic offer. I need a man like you. I need someone who I can depend on and who will have my back moving forward. I was hoping this would not be just a one-night thing, but that you would feel some debt towards me, and stick around."

"I'm not sure I fully understand. Like a relationship? I am not really the marrying kind." James said apprehensively, realizing that threat of marriage seemed to affect him more than the threat of zombie sex.

"Not a marriage, just...an arrangement. I have heard stories recently. The world is a bit chaotic right now and will be so for some time. I have heard of people like me disappearing. It sounds like a paranoid lunatics' fantasy, but there is talk, chatter. The most insane things being said are about what is happening with VINNI's. It may just be nonsenses, but will you promise to stay with me if I do this for you? Just till I feel safe?"

"Of course. Yes, that is not even a question you need to ask. I will protect you. At least until you feel safe on your own. I just need to see my sister off before she leaves for Cape May. The Colonel asked us to deliver a message to the President. She can do that for him."

Bethany was relieved. "Go let her know you will be staying here, as my guest. I will meet you back here in an hour. I will get us a motel room nearby. I also need to find some rope, duct tape and if possible some handcuffs."

"Wow, you do know the way to turn a guy on." James said sarcastically as he left to find Fiona.

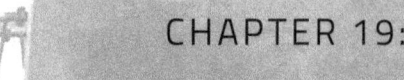

CHAPTER 19:

Kitchen Table Politics

He sat at the kitchen table flipping through the CCTV feeds on his laptop. The small boxes, nearly a dozen per view, appeared as small square windows into the world. He lingered on the stream in the six thousand range. You could choose your areas of the state to view by the bank of channels streaming the closed-circuit television cameras. Live video streams in the six thousand range covered Atlantic City. Much less violent than the three thousand range channels, which was the Newark region, but not as dull as the two thousand range, which covered mainly the newly opened colleges and universities. Still, every so often, you could catch a couple of horny collegiate getting it on late night, especially if the camera was panning at just the right time across the dorms. The lower numbered channels, channel one thousand and lower, were mainly residential neighborhoods. If you were interested in watching people walk their dogs and mow their lawns, those channels were for you. But to Benjamin, they were like visual Ambien.

Overnight, CCTV cameras had popped up like herpes. The administration seemed to place them on every pole that stood over six feet. To demonstrate transparency, they provided a live stream of the cameras right to the local cable channels. It was the ultimate reality TV. Unscripted, no directors, no writers and a captive audience of those unable or unwilling to leave New Jersey.

They say that cameras change people's behavior, thus the reason they will never be allowed in Supreme Court hearings, but these street cameras didn't so much change people, but allowed them to be whomever they wanted to be.

People began performing for the cameras. Really performing. They were not just changing their behaviors, they were celebrating and supersizing them. Those that wanted to have a street fight would still do so, but they would choose to fight on the street with the best camera angle. They would send word out through social media which camera bank the fight would be broadcast on and what time it would begin. It was appointment viewing at its worst.

The feeds were limited as they were just video, with no sound, but strippers soon realized they could promote their appearances at local clubs by providing previews on what-ever camera was closest to the flesh palace where they were dancing that evening. Atlantic City had the most dancer previews and that is where Benny would spend his search time. That is, when he was not dealing with his kids.

He was watching a blond, who had displayed shockingly poor judgment in her tattoo placement. She was writhing and dry humping a mailbox in front of Club Camel when Benny was startled by the knock on his back door.

He quickly closed the browser and warily approached the door. It was too late for unannounced visitors and it the fact that this visitor came to his back door meant it could only be one person, his neighbor Bruce.

Bruce entered the kitchen upon the door being opened, not waiting for his invite. He had a clipboard and pen in hand, which Benny knew the purpose of.

"Dude, I have been coming by your house every day for a week and can't find you. You take the kids on vacation or something?"

"No Bruce, just been very busy. Got your calls, your texts. Got your postings on my Facebook page. I know you are eager to talk with me." Benny sighed.

"Where are the kids, I have not seen them outside. You keeping in due to the zombies? I would too, I can't even let my dog out, and the basement is filling up with dog shit already, but damn, not going to put the dog outside when I can't keep an eye on him. Some fucking Skell will eat him. You know, they have been spotted in the neighborhood. I heard one was on this very block a couple days ago." Bruce said plopping his butt into the chair and slapping the clipboard on the kitchen table.

"Yep, I am keeping them close. You know, since Andrea passed, they are all I have." Benny said softly.

"Yeah, I get it man. But seriously, you need to go out and find another woman soon. Your balls must be backed up. Next woman you bang is going to get a fire hose. Am I right?" Bruce held up a high five that was un-responded to. He slowly, annoyed, brought his arm back down to his side.

"Where are the kids?" he asked, changing the subject.

"I need to feed them soon." Benny said with a weak smile hoping the hint would get his guest to cut his visit short.

"Yep, gotta feed those kids." Bruce said, not getting the hint.

"Penny and Lane." Benny said.

"What?" Bruce asked

"My kids, their names are Penny and Lane." Benny reminded.

"Oh, right, yeah, I forgot, you and Andrea were fucking flower children back in the day." Bruck snorted.

"Eh, more just into the classics. But I really do need to go, and Bruce, I know your petition is in support of Ronan, but I am just not going to sign it. I don't like that guy." Benny said, bracing himself for the blowback.

"What do you mean? We need to get Callahan out of office! The country is tearing itself apart with these fucking zombies. I mean, we did not start this, they're the violent ones. I mean, they were like you and I once, now they're violent lunatics. What the hell did we do to them? Why do they hate us?"

Benny laughed. "They don't hate us."

"They certainly don't love us. Those ain't love bites their giving people out there. They are ripping people to shreds." Bruce said, raising his voice and pointing out the kitchen window at nothing.

"They don't hate us any more than we hate the cows we eat. Do you think a mosquito hates you when it bites you? They are sick, they are different now. They are just following instincts to survive.

"Well, my instincts to survive are to kill them all. And the only way we are going to do that is by getting this President out of office and getting someone in that has the will to make things happen. I know this Ronan is a psycho. But he is a psycho that knows how to entertain. Knows how to speak to us and knows how to get shit done and I for one will be glad when we get Callahan out and this guy in." Bruce said loudly.

"Anyone that feels happy about this cyber thug and his army of internet assholes possibly taking over the presidency should not be so quick to celebrate a success. Callahan may be an amateur, but at least he was elected." Benny warned.

"Not to the presidency." Bruce countered.

"No, but he was elected to something. He was duly voted in by Americans. The fact that he is now president is not the point. Whether people like him or not is not the point. Whether he is even capable of doing the job is not the point." Benny was getting passionate.

"So, what is the fucking point?" Bruce asked.

"The point is, zombie apocalypse or not, we still have a functioning government, we are still a democracy. They pull him out, the trolls may be happy, but the rest of us will only see that the last living elected person from Washington was just dragged out because people are throwing tantrums and freaking out."

"One asshole is pulled out, another is put in. Big deal."

"The big deal is that asshole you put in is not going to represent anything. He is not elected, and even after he is dead and gone, every person following him in office will also be illegitimate. Once you fuck this democracy up, it stays fucked. There is no way to get the cherry back. It is broken. It may work, but it isn't ever going to be what we had. It is over. And I think...no, I believe, that anyone who is supporting this, advocating this, should be held responsible for the outcome. These celebrities I see running to support Ronan just because he turns them on and his perfectly chosen words are drooled over as if his speech is gently ear fucking them, are just as guilty. People are going to push back, perhaps violently." Benny finished, standing up and walking towards the back door to let his neighbor out.

Bruce was incensed. "Look, I know you are a bleeding heart and all, but I am not going to let these flesh eaters tear our country apart."

"So, you are going to tear it apart just because the asshole you want is not sitting on the throne right now? I think that will do a lot longer term damage than the infected." Benny said, turning the door knob.

"I fucking give up on you dude." Bruce snapped. "We got swammies taking over the neighborhood with their stupid robes and turbans. We have Mexicans renting houses next door to me, and now we have zombies roaming the streets and you don't give a fuck!" Bruce yelled.

Benny closed the door and walked over to the sink. He leaned forward and pulled the top window closed. He then reached for crank and began turning it to retract the lower window.

"What are you afraid of Benny?" Bruce yelled. "You don't want the swammies next door to hear me? Hey swammies, get back on your fucking magic carpet and fly back to Alibaba!" Bruce yelled.

Benny completed closing all the windows and walked back to ensure the back door was completely closed.

"What's a matter neighbor, you don't want the neighbors to hear what I am going to say?!" Bruce yelled.

"No, that's not it at all." Benny replied as he locked the door. "I don't what them to hear what you are going to scream."

Benny unlocked the kitchen pantry and let Penny and Lane out too feed.

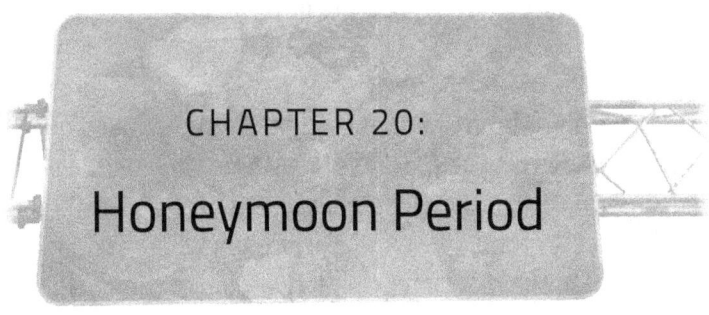

CHAPTER 20:

Honeymoon Period

Bethany had purposely chosen an out of the way no-tell motel to do the nasty.

As they paid for the room, she noticed a sign on the front desk sign informing guests that the motel is no longer affiliated with the Red Roof Inn chain. They apologized for any inconvenience this would cause. "Seriously?" she said to James. "How many corpses do you need to find stuffed under the mattress before you lose the coveted Red Roof Inn seal of approval?"

They walked from the check in window to their room, it became apparent that the room rates weren't the only cheap thing. They could hear sex, arguments and television programs as they passed in front of each room rooms. They were not quite sure what would happen post coitus, but they hoped it would not be loud. They arrived at room 51, the room's front door was barely two feet from the parking lot

James took care not to harm her as he strapped her wrists and ankles to the bed frame. They used thin rubber hoses, popular with junkies to tie themselves off before injection, as the restraint of choice. They felt the rubber would have the most "give" while still restraining Bethany once she began the change.

He did not want to use rope or handcuffs for fear her convulsions and escape attempts would damage her beautiful skin or break her bones. She lay there naked except for an oversized t-shirt, fully restrained, arms and legs akimbo. Under normal circumstances, this would be hot. The cheap, sleazy hotel, a stunningly beautiful woman who not only was consensual to the restraints, but demanding of them, were all the plot points of a memorable night, but as she said earlier, this had nothing to do with passion.

He held up a ball gag, used in S&M practice. She winced. "Let's hold off on that one for now," she asked. He did not argue and tossed it into the nightstand drawer. If nothing else, the next room guest who finds it can get adventurous.

James mounted her.

She had a fleeting memory of the previous hook up and what followed. It was just like remembering a dream upon waking up. Quick flashes of scenes imagined flittering away. What were so vivid moments earlier, dissipated like vapor.

And then it was over.

Neither of them would ever recall his encounter as a good lay. It is said that bad sex can become mechanical. This was worse, this was medicinal.

James sat in the cheap upholstered chair across from the still bound Bethany.

He puffed nervously on a cigarette.

"Those things will probably kill you," she said referring to the cancer stick.

"You will probably kill me," he replied trying to lighten the mood.

"Do you feel anything?" she asked.

"Not yet, do you?"

"Nothing yet." she said pensively.

"How long did it take with the other guy?" James asked.

"It was quick." she recalled with uncertainty. "I mean I remember the sex, and I remember laying there next to him, and then it gets a little hazy. Once I came too, he was...well, you know. Gone. For the most part. But I remember looking at the clock and thinking not much time had passed."

"Oh great." James said not making eye contact.

She smiled at the ridiculousness of the conversation. "Don't get self-conscious. You were fine. Look it was a weird situation, no girl can expect a guy to..."

"Ok, enough. But why is nothing happening. I mean, did he do anything I didn't do?" James probed.

Bethany could not believe it was she, the one tied up naked, who was trying to put him at ease. "Look that guy and I were kind of in a different mindset at the time. Neither of us had an agenda. We were just trying to get off." she paused. "We weren't trying to cure cancer."

"Hey, funny. You're funny. You should do stand up." he said getting annoyed.

"It's called a personality you should consider getting one someday." she teased him. "When you're not the hot chick, or even the doable chick, you are forced to develop other traits, like a sense of humor. Usually a caustic one to deal with the daily insults lobbed your way. It is how I coped through high school. And college. And pretty much life up until just recently, it was the only way I could compete."

"Well, look at you now." James said with a wave of his hand bringing attention to her newly fit bod. He gave her a once over again with his eyes. "You became the beautiful swan."

"Yeah, check me out," she said rolling her eyes. "I'm on a filthy mattress, in a sleazy motel room, tied up like a deer on the hood of a car. I truly do feel beautiful."

James spurt out in laughter. She was funny. And besides the fact that she was probably going to turn into a cannibal shortly, he was enjoying his time with her.

"You ain't the only one with a sob story. To be honest, even with the filthy mattress and you being tied up and possibly going all savage on me, this is probably the best date I have had in a decade." James lamented. Her eyebrow rose when she realized he referred to this evening as a date.

They sat in silence for a few moments.

"Want to paint my toenails?" she asked. "I have polish in my purse. I really can't think of anything else we can do with me in this position."

"Still nothing?" he asked.

"Nope," was her disappointed response.

"But with the first guy, it happened pretty quickly huh?"

She could not believe he was going back to this again. "Look, don't get jealous, he was in the past, I did not even know you then. No need to be insecure about my past lovers. Besides, he's dead. I ate him remember?" she said hoping to put this to rest.

"Should we do it again?" he asked.

"Do you want to?" she replied.

"Do YOU want to?" he asked.

"Hey, I got nowhere else to be right now, kind of tied up," she said motioning to her bound arms. "And to tell you the truth, I think you deserve a second chance."

They were both startled by a knock at the door. They exchanged looks. The knock came again.

"Hello?" James asked.

There was no answer, but a third knock, this time harder.

"Housekeeping!" the female voice announced.

"Come back later." James said.

There was another knock. James looked through the peep-hole and saw the side of the woman's face up against door.

She knocked again. "Housekeeping!" she repeated, a little louder.

"Do NOT let her in here with me like this!" Bethany demanded.

James fiddled with the chain on the door. "Why not, the room is a mess, let's have her give a quick vacuum."

"Don't you dare, you asshole!" She laughed and wriggled against her restraints.

"Come on, perhaps she'll leave us some chocolates on the pillow. Who knows, maybe she wants to join in for a threesome?"

"Stop it you moron!" Beth said, knowing full well that he was not serious.

James removed the chain, and fidgeted with the knob as if he were going to unlock the door, he let her wriggle in panic for a bit before he ended the charade.

"OK, I am opening the door now!" he said in a 'They're coming to get you Barbara' tone. "But here, I will cover your shame." he said and playfully threw the extra sheet over her, completely covering her face and body. James thought about jumping on top of the wriggling white sheet covered lump. He had not been this playful since, well, ever.

The levity did not last long, as the moment he let go of the still locked doorknob, the door was kicked open and a 9mm pistol was pointed at James face.

The man holding the gun pushed the housekeeping woman into the room with his free hand as she fell to the ground cowering.

"Well, well, what do we have here?" the man sneered. James looked over at the helpless Bethany, covered by the sheet; she had gone completely still.

He then looked beyond the gun that was inches from his face to see a white van just outside the hotel room door. Another man was standing at the open sliding side door and was preparing something inside.

The gunman stepped into the room and closed the door behind him.

The maid began praying quietly in Spanish.

The man pointed his gun at her and in mock Spanish commanded. "You, Senorita, move! Andale! Get into the bathroom. Bathroom!" he said in an attempt at Spanish. The frightened woman understood what he meant and complied.

The man then turned his attention on the outline of Bethany under the sheet, yet kept the gun pointing at James. "Don't worry honey, I see you under there." He turned to look at James again.

"Look dude, I hate to burst your bubble here, but if you thought you were getting laid tonight, it ain't happening. It may not seem like it right now, but I may have just saved your life. This chick," he said with a nod to Bethany, "she ain't a real chick."

James gave no response.

"I mean, she is a chick, like she isn't a dude or tranny or anything. She's infected. She has the same disease that is creating all the zombies out there, only she's what we call, a carrier. She does not look like a Skell, but she is one. And if you had stuck your dick in that, you would have been one too. That is, if she did not eat you first. We call this type Pillow Biters. Because after you finish banging them, they will bite your throat out before your head leaves the pillow."

James continued to stay silent and to ensure his face gave off no clues that this was not unique news to him.

"So, pal, what I am going to do is put you in the bathroom just for a little bit. We are going to take her out of here and then we are going to leave. I know this sounds crazy, but we are doing you a huge fucking favor right now. So go in the bathroom, lock the door, keep your mouth shut and wait about fifteen minutes. Who knows, maybe the maid in there will give you a rub and tug," he cracked.

The man then turned to the bed and whipped off the sheets. "OK, miss, time to go," he began but stopped mid-sentence when he realized she was bound to the bed.

James lunged forward but the man quickly turned his gun back towards James forehead.

"Holy shit. Either you are into some weird shit, or, more likely, it seems you knew what she was."

The man backed up towards the door, he opened it slightly and turned his head just enough to project his voice outside by keep his eye and gun trained on James.

"Hey Mr. Pinskey, looks like we got a guy trying to get free health care!"

"You know what to do." Pinskey called back. Sullivan recognized the bastard's voice.

"Yep, on it," the gunman called back and shut the room door again. He walked towards James while reaching into his inside jacket pocket to retrieve something.

James scoured the room, looking for a weapon. The man got within a foot of James and pulled a small white card from his pocket and handed it to James.

"Look, we run a little business here." The man explained. "I don't think you were trying to move in on it, but I do think you were trying to get something for nothing. There is no such thing as a free lunch, this isn't socialism, this is capitalism. You call this number, and we will instruct you how much money to bring and where to bring it. Then we will provide you a little lady just like this. We take care of everything. You get laid, you get cured, and then you leave. Because once you leave, these sweet young things turn into man-eaters. I mean seriously. We feed this creature some human flesh, someone who probably had it coming to them anyway, and bing bang boom, they are back to normal. Hose 'em down and they are ready for their next customer. There are other options as well, but to be honest pal, I don't think you could afford it. So, I am not taking away your cure, I am just telling you this is like concierge medicine. You need to pay and we don't accept insurance. Understand? Now, I just need you to step in to that bathroom for a few minutes."

James knew if he let them take her, he would never see her again. There was no way he was going to leave her to that type of slavery, that type of inhumanity. He took one step forward, then it hit him.

Like a massive punch to the stomach, but one that came from the inside. Then a second one. He felt like a freight train was barreling down his lower intestines.

He ran to the bathroom where the poor maid was standing in the bathtub. James threw his ass onto the toilet seat and all hell broke loose.

"Jesus pal, you really are 'shit your pants' scared, aren't you? I was not really going to shoot you." The gunman said as he slammed the bathroom door closed with his foot, his right hand occupied by the gun, his left holding his nose.

James tried to get up, but again, the pain in his stomach doubled him over and what burst forth from his lower half was a hurricane of incontinence. He heard screaming, but was not sure if it was coming from Bethany, the maid or his own pained sphincter.

He flushed, but a CSX freight rain of shit followed. He flushed again, and repeated, only this time it was more like the AMTRAK express. Just as fast, but not as brutish.

He flushed a third time and looked over at the poor Spanish woman cowering in the fetal position in the tub. She looked at him and then at the toilet as if his ass needed an exorcist.

James regained his composure, but a full fifteen minutes had passed since he became king of the porcelain thrown. They could be miles away. He opened the bathroom door, but the gunman had wedged the nightstand in-between the door and the closet. He pushed once more, driving the desk against the closet sliding door till the doors came free of their tracks. One more shove and the door was open enough to free himself. He ran out of the room and saw the van was no longer parked in front. James began towards his own car, only to realize he did not have his car keys. As he turned around to return to the room, he saw what looked like the white van. It was parked in an odd position, just on the other side of the lot, as if it has simply rolled backwards from its original parking space in front of their hotel door.

James ran towards the vehicle. Not seeing anyone in the driver seat, he assumed they must have switched cars. Or worse, both men were raping her in the back of the van. James reached the van, grabbed the side door and slid it open so hard it bent the frame. He was about to charge in and beat the two men to a bloody pulp, but it was too late.

They were already bloody pulp. Blood, skin, intestines, bone and god knows what else were strewn around the van. In the center sat a blood-soaked Bethany; quietly weeping.

James reached his hand out and put it gently on her bloody shoulder.

She looked up at him, her eyes still bright and beautiful through the crimson gore covering her face.

"Sometimes it just takes a girl a little longer to finish," she said with a weak smile.

CHAPTER 21:

Foreign Contribution

Daniel Sullivan walked into what was once the catering kitchen of the hotel, which had now been converted into a bio safety laboratory. He saw Dr. Woodrow Colman conversing with two men in lab coats. They were taking turns peering into a microscope and discussing what they viewed.

Once Woodrow had begun his web broadcast using Colonel Tindall's laptop, the contractors had his position pinpointed. They found him still at the house he had been hiding in since fleeing FOB Prince. Tindall and his men were gone, but Woodrow and his colleague from the subterranean PCRC Lab, Dr. Mohammed Ghazi, were still there waiting for the contractors to arrive.

Daniel sat himself on a wheeled stool and rolled himself over to the scientists, giving Woodrow a painful kick in the ass as he came to a stop. "What are you looking at nerds? You jerk off in a dish and checking out your own sperm that will never get close to a real girl?"

"It's fucking high school all over again." Woodrow murmured.

Mohammed did not know what to make of this man and his insults.

"I am going to get some coffee. You need anything?" Woodrow asked the other two scientists. They nodded they did not, and Woodrow walked out of the room.

"Hey waitress, you're not going to take my drink order?" Sullivan called to him but was ignored.

"So," Sullivan said, turning his attention to Mohammed. "You are the Mohammed I have heard about."

The other man in the lab coat, not wanting to be the next of Daniels targets, quickly made his way to the other side of the lab.

Daniel continued. "I hear you are the one that saved my little buddy Woodrow back at the lab. I appreciate that, usually it was me and my brothers getting him out of trouble. I appreciate the assist."

Mohammed gave a courteous nod and flipped through the pages on his clipboard.

"He said he was about to pull the plug on himself when you came back for him." Daniel continued.

Mohammed cast a wary eye towards the man. "Yes, it's true, I guess."

"Came up from under the floorboard panels, as he told me." Sullivan recalled.

"Yes". Mohammed replied without elaboration.

"What happened to the other scientists?" Daniel queried.

"Excuse me?" Mohammed replied, returning his attention to the microscope.

"The other scientists that were with you, in the lab. I don't think you will find them looking through that spy glass."

"I am not sure what you are asking me." Mohammed replied, still not looking up.

"Woodrow told me that he was there with a couple of you Middle Eastern types. Yet, seems none of them made it out of the place. Just you. Of course, you and Woodrow. Oh, also that fat security guard. Not sure how his wide ass made it out of there alive, but I know Woodrow made it out because of you."

"I am glad that I could save him."

"But, where were the other scientists? The ones that were part of your research team? Had they taken a quick trip to Mecca the day of the raid?"

"I doubt it. None of us were permitted to leave the facility. At all." Mohammed answered. "I am sure they were still there when it began."

"I'm sure also." Daniel replied. "I was just kidding about the Mecca thing. I know they were still there because we found their bodies. What was left of their bodies. Pretty bad shape. A little bit burned, a little bit eaten, and a little bit melted by thermite."

"That is truly a shame." Mohammed replied sadly.

"A little bit shot in the head." Daniel continued, noticing the scientist's hands stopped fidgeting with the microscope dial.

Mohammed continued to peer into the microscope. After a few seconds, he again began moving the dial. "There was a lot of shooting. I was alone when it all began. I was just trying to get out when I saw Dr. Coleman.

"And again, you popped up through the floor panels. Like the Viet Cong used to pop out of the ground to take out our boys." Sullivan commented.

"You fought in Viet Nam?" Mohammed said sarcastically. "You are holding up quite well."

"Nah, I was never in any real action in Asia, well, not officially." Daniel said in full braggadocio manner, leaning back on his stool and making air quotations with his fingers when he said officially. "All of my official military action was over in your neck of the woods. The sandbox."

"I am sure you were never in my country. My neck of the woods." Mohammed replied making his own air quotes.

"It was all the fucking same to me. Just like all of you were the same to me. I was just brought there to do a job, and I did it, I did it exceptionally well."

"Yes," Mohammed replied finally lifting his head from the lab device. "I am sure you killed many brown people. After all they are all the same, correct?"

"Now don't get angry with me." Daniel replied defiantly. "I did not want to be over there. Not like I enjoyed wearing forty pounds of gear while running around in heat that should not exist anywhere but the surface of the sun. If you fuckers would just chill out a bit, we would not have to come over there."

"Chill out?" Mohammed asked in disbelief. "And your countries foreign policy has nothing to do with any of the problems over there?"

"Sure, blame the Americans. I have no idea how to communicate with your types. For us, your whole region is like an angry ocean. Only that ocean is filled with violence in murder. And the waves of violence keep crashing up on other people's shores. Crash, a huge wave of violence." Daniel said, using his arm to simulate a wave making a curl and crashing down onto his other arm which symbolized the beach. "Crash, a wave of terror. Crash, a wave of violence," he continued. "Hour after hour, day after day, year after year, that ocean keeps churning and those waves keep crashing. Then, someone walks on that beach and spits into that ocean, and the entire sea erupts at the insult. The waves come crashing even harder and harder until whomever originated this perceived insult is laid low by the crashing waves and sucked into the sea to his death. The ocean then goes back to its steady state, satisfied that it destroyed the originator of this undeserved slight. Yet those waves keep coming. Crash, a wave of violence. Crash, a wave of terror. Yet it was that one slight, that one spit, that was the cause of all the problems."

The two men looked at each other with mutual disdain.

Mohammed thought of the adage about wresting with a pig. He felt he would get just a little dirtier. "What you don't understand is that you don't understand. That is it, plain and simple. You think democracy is the greatest gift you could bestow upon our lands, our people. You love your democracy, we understand that, but to be honest, I doubt much of your country even understands how it works. What is involved to make it function.

"Democracy to you is like the internet. You don't know how it works, but you love it. You know you pay a monthly bill, which gives you access to something of tremendous value. The internet, the web. Facebook, Netflix, videos, porno sites. You don't know how it works, or how it is delivered to you, or what it is comprised of. But you know you like it.

Just like democracy. You pay your tax bill, and you get democracy.

"Democracy, like the internet, can be used, abused, or wasted.

"When I was in university, I only had two hours a day at which time I could access the school computer and get online. One hour in the morning and one at night. If I did not get to sign up sheet early enough in the day, I may not get it at all. And when I did get on it, I learned organic chemistry. I learned biology. I read and wrote papers on new scientific discoveries. I used those precious moments with the internet wisely. I did not take them for granted. Waste them on social media, posting about my lunch, watching videos of cats or seeking out porno."

Daniel smiled, as he had not heard it referred to as porno since his grandmother yelled at him after finding an old playboy under his bed.

"I could not look at those images anyway, as the computers were restricted and most websites blocked.

Now, I am here in America, I have as much internet as I want. So, what do I do with it? Do I play Angry Birds, and binge-watch Sopranos? Do I research and study?" He raised his lips and hands, "Actually a little of both. So, I am approaching the internet much like you approach democracy. You enjoy it, but you don't think about it, you are willing to look at whatever is coming next that may replace it that you could enjoy more, but if it does go away, you will feel as if a hole has appeared in your life."

"So, what's your point Jambi?" Daniel sniped.

Mohammed brushed off the name-calling. "My point, is that you feel you can just take what is good and working for you and impose it on other cultures. Perhaps our people are not so looking for a life as loose and free as yours. Some people feel happy and secure under a strong leader, one that makes all the decisions, and one that makes you feel pride in your homeland. A leader that may have to take harsh, sometimes brutal, actions against dissenters. But sometimes it is for the common good. In my country, we have a leader who was not elected, but I can still work, make a living, and pursue my goals. I have a friend who lives under a Sultanate, yet he too has freedoms."

"Yeah, but you can't choose your own leaders. Neither you nor your children have any chance of rising to lead your country." Daniel said.

"You are asking if my children will I ever grow up to be the president of my country? No, no chance. But honestly, when you were a child, did you think you could grow up to be president. Did you think anyone you were growing up with could be president?" Mohammed asked.

"Well I got you there Abu. You see, Patrick Callahan and I go back to grade school, and sure enough, today he is the President of these here United States. How do you like them apples?"

Mohammed stood there smirking. "Well Mr. Sullivan, it looks like you do have me there. I guess you win this argument."

Dan was all puffed up. "I win every argument. I am an American and we kick ass. Might makes right. There's your lesson for the day *Mohammed*."

Woodrow returned with his coffee mug full and gave the now silent men a wary look. "What are you two talking about?" he asked nervously.

The two men took a moment to continue their silent staring war.

"Nothing." Daniel said. "I was just letting the Mo-man here how much I appreciated him saving your ass."

Daniel turned to Mohammed. "And I truly am grateful." he said with actual sincerity and turned back to Woodrow "Other than that, we were not talking about anything of importance, nothing that needs to be talked about any further. You two nerds have fun playing with your beakers." Daniel said beginning to take his leave but then stopped for one more comment.

"Oh, Mohammed," Daniel said, getting his name correct for the first time. "I will speak to the President. I know you were brought here against your will, so as soon as you are ready to go home, just say the word and we will give clearance for an international flight. It will take you to wherever you want to go." And with that magnanimous gesture, Daniel left the men to their work.

Woodrow turned to Mohammed. "Are you ok? He can be an asshole, but he is as loyal as they come. He knows what you did for me and will look out for you. It's good to have someone watching your back."

"Yes, I agree." Mohammed said lowering his head to view the blood samples under the microscope. "And when you do what we do, it is good to have someone watching your back."

CHAPTER 22:

Identity Politics

A look of disgust appeared on Majesty's face as Lars entered the room. He returned the favor with an equally hate filled glare.

"I see your dog is here, so I will leave you to let it lick your boots." Majesty sneered.

"I thought I smelled the sub human stench of Jewishness when I entered." Lars gave his typical response.

"Oh, gee, a Nazi that hates Jews, you are so original Lars. Well I know your kind hated gypsies also, well I am a bit of a gypsy and I am going to tell you your future. You will eventually end up in prison, where all the idiots end up, and your big black, homosexual cellmate is going to rape you and he will pump your ass so full of his sperm that it will leak from your eyes. Eventually you will die either of AIDS, or your rectum will be so damaged, it will simply just fall out."

"Yeah, well you're probably going to die of cunt cancer." Lars sputtered, incapable of achieving anything better to fling at her.

She stood looking at him, her face a combination of disgust and confusion as to how to even respond to that. She shook her head and glided out of the room.

"Cunt cancer?" Ronan asked.

"Man, why is she here. Why do you stay with her? I understood when we were in California and you two lived in her parent's basement, but you don't need her anymore."

"I stay with her because she is stronger than I am, stronger that most of us. She is ruthless. These vegans will deprive themselves from eating an animal, but will slit a man's throat and then sit down for a tofu breakfast." Ronan explained. "Plus, we had some great sex in her parent's basement."

"Really, I thought great sex was forbidden in Jewish households." Lars cracked.

Ronan smiled. "And I stayed with you because you made me smile. It is one of the things I will miss most about you."

Lars went cold, he felt a pang in his stomach and almost immediately began to sweat.

"...Miss me?"

"Don't worry, I am sorry, that came out wrong. It is just that I am breaking up the band. I need to enter the political process. I need you to go in another direction to keep GRASS alive, but without my involvement."

Ronan took out his phone and texted Majesty asking her to return to the room.

"How can you just take a group like ours and make it legit? The people, the sheep people, the police. They will never accept us. They will crucify us." Lars said still not believing what he was hearing.

"What we have done was nothing more than a bit of aggressive political action. Community organizing you may say. Getting the message out, rallying the troops, mobilizing the resistance. All the typical crap you hear other politicians say. It is just that we took it to the next level. It may not be popular. It may be offensive to some. But it is protected speech; just like burning the flag or killing a cop. We are expressing our political frustrations. Who are they to judge us? Anyone who tries to cast judgment on our behavior is obviously a racist, sexist, homophobic, antiemetic, Islamophob."

"Um, Ronan, don't we hate all those classifications of people also?" Lars reminded

"We do when it suits our purpose. For now, we self-identify with the oppressed minority. And that is where we will build our candidacy." Ronan the statesman explained.

"Candidacy?"

Majesty walked back in. "What's the matter, your dog try to hump your leg?" she said referring to Lars.

"I have decided I am going to run for President." Ronan announced to the room.

Laughter was the response from Lars and Majesty.

"I am serious, we have gained all we can gain on our current path, it is time we joined the political process. Just like Sin Fein, the PLO and other organization that had their start in violence, eventually, they reach a zenith and must join in."

"But, you? You're a murderer." Lars reminded.

"All presidents are murderers. They send men off to die in worthless, unwinnable wars, is that not murder?" Ronan countered.

"Yeah, but you murdered people before you ran for president." Lars replied.

"George Washington was a General before he was President, you don't think he killed people?" Ronan said as a counterpoint.

"Probably, on the battlefield, but you're not a soldier, you shot people in the face. Unarmed people. In fact, you killed more than three people that I know of, and on separate occasions, which would categorize you as a serial killer. It is the very definition of the term 'Serial Killer.'"

"What's you fucking point, *Lawrence*?" Ronan snapped, getting annoyed.

Lars did not like to be called by his real name and felt he was being disrespected.

"So, what do you think we are all going to do, become your fucking political advisors?" Lars asked referring to Majesty and himself.

"Speak for yourself asshole." Majesty interrupted. "I will be the first lady."

"Great," Lars threw his hands up in frustration. "A first lady who killed more people than the serial killer President. Great fucking campaign slogan. Vote for me, or you'll be next."

"Lars," Ronan said, in a calm voice that was not meant to calm but to get his troubled sidekick to shut up. "I believe your services are no longer needed today."

Lars became nervous. He looked over his shoulder to ensure Majesty was not sneaking up behind him with a knife.

"What, you think you are going to just get rid of me now.

"In ancient times, a leader usually killed those that had killed for him. You see, once they rise to power, they know what they those that have been loyal to him are capable of. If they could help bring him to power, they could bring him down as well, or perhaps switch their murderous loyalties to the leader's opponents. But no Lars, I am not going to kill you, and

I will make it clear to all our followers that you are leaving the movement on your own accord, and are not to be challenged or threatened in any way.

"The old G.R.A.SS is no more. Our new political organization will rise. We will challenge this President, we will force a new election, and we will win." Ronan leaned towards Lars. "And at that point, when I have achieved my new role, you can once again join me by my side. But for now, I must do this on my own."

CHAPTER 23:

Ancient Régime

Over the course of the following months, Ronan's pervasive cyber stalking of the President had moved from annoyance to a true political threat. While no one had yet seen the man in public, Ronan's near hourly appearances on Twitter, Snapchat and other social and media platforms had become a national addiction. His taunts, commentary and pronouncements of his own political ambitions had made him a darling of the media. Reporters had already grown bored of reporting on the zombie apocalypse and were seeking new stories. Ronan was providing them a nonstop tirade of conspiracy theories and orchestrated outrage. The Callahan administration had gone silent and was overwhelmed with the day-to-day managing of both the country and the Skell pandemic. It left them no time to even prepare news releases updating the press on their activities. This void was filled by Ronan's pronouncements as to why he was a better choice to run the country.

The reporters, and much of a fascinated nation, clicked on links that were tweeted out new each day, allowing him to play hide and seek with the administration, law enforcement and the contractors, all of whom had compelling cause to want Ronan shut down.

His tweets over the past week had telegraphed a major political announcement to be presented by Ronan, and at noon on Monday, the people diligently followed the link in his previous tweet to view his pre-recorded video announcement.

"Good people of our beloved homeland." The video began. The video displayed what was presumably Ronan, wearing his usual rubber cow mask that he had worn on all previous videos and photo appearances to mask his identity. "Our President has said that I am afraid to show my face". The cow said to the sheep.

Ronan reached up and pulled the rubber mask off his head and tossed it aside.

As he revealed his face for the first time to his viewing public, there was a collective gasp across the shallow regions of America.

Blonde-haired, blue-eyed, unblemished skin covering his perfect features.

Arian features, is a description that would have been used during a different time.

"Our so called elected officials initiated this virus in hopes that they would destabilize our country just long enough for them to become kings. He, our unelected President, sits today in Cape May, the new center of power, surrounded by his hired thugs, The Contractors as they are called, his own version of the Roman Legion.

"Yet he calls for my arrest. Me, his political opponent.

"He fancies himself a dictator. Is this what America has become, a place where rulers call for the arrest of their political opponents? Or will he forgo the arrests and just have his contractors assassinate me?

"It is he, the false president that should be arrested. All the others Washington politicians like him have already met the fate they deserved, devoured by one another, much like starving rats would devour their own aboard an abandoned, sinking ship.

"Think of the enormity of what has befallen our great country.

"Nearly two hundred and fifty years ago, a handful of men and women got together and formed an entity that did not exist prior. A new democracy.

"That new democracy was born first from their minds and imaginations. Then from their labor and sacrifice. And finally, from their blood and flesh. And as time passed, it was handed on to the next generation with only one request asked of the recipient; keep it alive.

"The only thing that each succeeding generation who received this gift, this democracy, had to achieve was to keep it alive.

"And it was kept alive for nearly two hundred and fifty years.

"When we, all of us alive today, were born, it was still alive.

"That was all they had to do, keep it alive.

"And it was kept alive.

"Until now.

"Someone let it die.

"Imagine having a child, raising it, putting it in the care of hundreds of other people throughout that child's life; teachers, bus drivers, car pool, coaches and family. Each of those you entrusted had one central mission, keep that child alive while it is in their care.

"Then, after years, your child is handed to someone, someone whom you trusted. And that someone let your child die. One request, keep it alive, and they failed. That is how I feel about those that have let this democracy die.

"To some, it will be of no great matter. They were not invested in the success of their country. They felt disenfranchised, even hostile, to our great democracy.

"But to those of us that understand what it must have been like there at the very beginning, it is not something we can simply forgive. We must come to the realization that no matter what others have started for us, or what we ourselves have started for our future decedents, it is up to the future recipients to keep what we create alive. And now nothing is certain."

Ronan continued talking making sure he hit all the right buzz words that would pull at the heart strings. He spoke about the environment, animal rights, and the power of the collective.

Ronan spoke about the dangers of the Skell virus and the need for a compassionate resolution for managing the infected.

He won over all the media and all the news organizations. It didn't matter what he did in the past and it didn't matter what he'll do in the future, for right now, they had found their Golden Boy and they were going to follow is commands.

After thirty minutes, he completed his salvo at the establishment.

"So, I am asking that you vote for me as your next President.

"I will create a new form of government

"Our previous federal government has outgrown its usefulness.

"No longer will Washington be filled with white stone buildings housing agencies that served as nothing more than federally sanctioned warehouses for the greedy, the lazy and the ignorant.

"The governing bodies of this land, institutions, that were once populated by our so called elected officials, have reached end of life. They are not forests that require re-planting after a wildfire. They were petrified forests, filled with rotting, infested deadwood which needed to be burned away to make way for the new growth. Our growth. The growth of GRASS. My name is Ronan, just Ronan, and I am asking for you to vote for me. No, not vote. I am asking for you to DEMAND that I become your new President."

CHAPTER 24:

Growing the Base

"So, Sami just tweeted out her endorsement for you." Majesty squealed with delight.

"Wow, that is great, who the hell is Sami?" Ronan asked

"She is a singer, you know SAMI!" Majesty explained. "She is the first non-binary solo artist with a hit single." Majesty was in fan girl mode as she read the news from her phone.

"What the hell is non-binary?" Ronan asked. "Is that like the metric system? Who gives a shit, Canada uses metric system and they suck."

"No, non-binary means she has no sex." Majesty informed as if she were explaining the earth is round.

"So, she is a virgin?" Ronan asked

"No, I mean she has no gender."

"Lost me." Ronan replied.

"She is not a girl or a boy." Majesty continued, unsure as to why he did not understand this concept.

"You said she. She is a singer. So, she is not a her?" Ronan asked.

"No, I mean, they." Majesty corrected.

"So, she is a part of a group?" Ronan asked.

"No, she sings alone." Majesty replied.

"You just said THEY?" Ronan snapped, getting frustrated with this advanced calculus Majesty was throwing at him.

"I don't know what her fucking pronoun is, ok, just deal with the fact that we have our first celebrity endorsement." Majesty snapped at the clueless man.

"Great, so we have the sixteen-year-old demographic. They can't even vote." Ronan said dismissively.

"Well he/she is going to promote you at all his/her concerts. The kids worship her, and will tell their parents about you." Majesty said trying to get everyone as excited as she was.

"I thought people were now worshiping the infected now?" Ronan asked. "I guess you gotta worship something; God, government, celebrity, money, pick your poison."

"Uh oh." Majesty said staring intently at the screen on her phone.

"What's up?" Ronan asked.

"She just tweeted that the corporate fascists are trying to turn us all into Skells so they can control and kill us. She ended her text with a hashtag #AllLivesMatter."

"Yeah, so? I thought our followers were all about platitudes?" Ronan mocked.

"Now the black lives matter folks are tweeting back, going after her for diminishing their tagline." Majesty said worried.

Majesty continued staring intently at the screen while she explained the play by play of the observed tweet war to Ronan.

"Ok, she is correcting. She apologized and posted that she is for all lives.

"Whoa, now her twitter stream is blowing up, everyone is accusing her of being a pro-lifer.

"Ok she is correcting again. She tweeted that she is pro-choice and that abortion is protected in the constitution."

"I don't think that's accurate?" Ronan commented.

"Well she also spelled constitution wrong." Majesty updated.

"Oh crap, they are attacking her over her referencing the constitution. They are calling her tea party, tea bagger, ok, um, trying to keep up with the retweet replies. Something about constitution written by slave-owners.

"Ok, she is correcting, she just tweeted out a quote referencing Gandhi, also spelled wrong.

"Nope, that did not work, they are accusing her of cultural appropriation.

"Ok, now she is, she is coming on line. Oh yikes!" Majesty put her hand over her mouth. "She just lived streamed her own suicide."

Ronan stood up to go get lunch. "Maj", he said, "favor please, no more celeb endorsements. OK?"

CHAPTER 25:

Crossing the Aisle

Lars sat, uncomfortably, in the leather chair. The hunting lodge where he had travelled for this meeting represented everything he despised, yet privately aspired to possess. Trophy animal heads on the wall interspersed with black and white framed posters from The Godfather, Goodfellas and The Sopranos. An oak wood bar displaying expensive bottles of scotch and vodka. Large cigar holder type ashtrays lay on the tables.

In front of Lars sat Gary Ragu, current boss of the largest organized crime family in New Jersey.

Lars had sought Ragu out, as in his twisted mind, if Ronan was Hitler, then Ragu was as close to Mussolini as he could find. Lars had come with an offer. He had heard that Ragu's organization was unhappy about the instability that Ronan was causing. There could only be one devil in hell, and Ragu wanted to ensure he was top of the criminal food chain. President Callahan was a known-known, and that Ronan was a known-unknown.

Lars offered Ragu his services in removing this unknown.

Lars explained that although he had been cast out of the fold, he felt that he could still find and get close to Ronan.

After a long pause, Ragu leaned back in his leather chair and began to relay his thoughts aloud to Ronan.

"This thing of ours, this organization." Ragu began waving his right hand in a small circle as if to signify everything that surrounded them. "Think of it like an ocean. A vast and deep ocean that counts on all its inhabitants to contribute. My purpose in this ocean is to serve as a coral reef. Quietly, patiently, over years and decades, building an ecosystem. An ecosystem that will sustain life in this ocean for the future and beyond."

Ragu pointed with his chin to Little V, who was standing ominously over Lar's right shoulder. "Vito here, he is a shark. An apex predator. Unlike the coral reef, whose growth is so slow and stealthy, that it cannot be witnessed by human eyes, the shark never stops moving. The shark never stops hunting, feeding, moving on to find his next prey. The shark also supports this ocean, by defending the reef from predators that could cause it harm. The shark, with his ravenous appetite, also keeps the population in check, which helps keep the ecosystem in balance. We need both the stable, life giving reef and the quick and brutal shark to have a balanced ecosystem."

Lars nodded, but did not fully comprehend.

Ragu continued. "If you want to be part of this ocean, this organization, this family; we have to ensure you are a proper fit. Not something that will upset the balance. Everyone must contribute."

Lars imagined the Skells out there, killing and eating and killing and eating. Were they currently the dominant apex predator in this world?

Lars waited for a second, making sure Ragu was finished and that it was his turn to speak. "I feel I can contribute. But may I ask, what am I in this ocean?" Lars asked.

Ragu took a drag from his cigarette and blew the smoke directly at Ronan. "Right now, you are a catfish, a bottom feeder. Your role is to clean up the shit left by others in the ocean."

Lars hated that he had to sit there and metaphorically, eat the shit that was being shovel his way. But Ronan put him in this position. He climbed his way up the GRASS organization, and he could do it again with this one. Lars nodded the affirmative to Ragu as to signal he understood and accepted what his role would be. "I can do that." he said.

Gary Ragu raised his eyes to Little V as if to say, 'You take it from here.' Ragu stood up and left the room without a goodbye or final glance at Lars.

Little V walked across the room and over to the bar. He passed by all the expensive liquor and opened the small fridge and pulled out a bottle of beer. He twisted open the bottle with his large, mitt sized hands and tossed the cap onto the bar, not offering or asking Lars if he also would like an adult beverage.

Little V's name was misleading. Little V was a massive, muscle bound, tattooed hulk. His jet-black hair and wife beater tee shirt shouted his origins. Lars's eyes took notice of the man's physique. If only his skin were pale, his eyes blue and his hair blond, he would make the perfect Arian man. Little V always appeared as if he had just finished a hardcore workout session at the gym. He was always pumped, always flexed, always breathing like a barely contained bull. He was the human manifestation of a steroid rage.

"Ragu said you have a lot to offer." V said, standing in front of Lars, but not taking advantage of the seat that was directly opposite his guest.

"Yes, I hope so." Lars answered.

"Hope? Fuck hope, leave hope to Obama. I want to hear that you KNOW son!" V replied.

"Yes, I KNOW I have a lot to offer you." Lars replied unconvincingly.

"Our associates have a special relationship with the current administration." V continued, choosing to stand over his seated guest rather than sit and be eye to eye. "We have contracts that we want to ensure continue long into the future. These trucks that are used for picking up the zombies are leased by the government from a company owned by Ragu. The facilities that operate to keep them freaks contained are cleaned and managed by another within our family of companies. Ragu said you can assist in ending the candidacy of our Presidents challenger, this little hippy prick Ronan. We are supporters of the current administration and we don't want regime change. Understand?"

Lars shifted in his seat, he began to stand up to be on par with V, but the large man quickly put out his hand to signify Lars was to remain seated.

Lars began, "Well yes, Ragu..."

"Excuse me?! You are getting pretty familiar already by calling him 'Ragu.'"

Lars backtracked. "I apologize, I meant Gary..."

"Gary? You feel that you two are on a first name basis? Again, you seem to be taking privilege in your brief, and I do mean brief, association with my boss."

"I apologize." Lars said again.

"Stop fucking apologizing, just show some respect here." V said, raising his voice to the increasingly flustered Lars.

"Ummm. Mr....." It was then that he realized he did not know Gary's last name. "Mr. Gary told me..."

"Mr. Gary? What are you, a fucking Mexican? Only wetbacks call him Mr. Gary!" V spat out, completely stumping Lars as to how to continue.

"Ummm...I approached...Your employer. I told him that I was formally associated with the prior organization of Ronan." Lars stammered.

"I know that. Ragu was impressed, he asked me to work with you to move this ball forward. And when I say work with you, I mean to say, manage you. You can get rid of this fucking prick that thinks he can be President, correct?"

"Yes, I believe I can, I hope so." Lars said.

"Nah nah nah, that is not what Ragu said. He said you CAN get rid of him. He did not say you *believed* you can or you *hoped* you can. He said you CAN get rid of him!"

"Well, of course I think I can, I just...." Lars tried to reply.

V interrupted again. "Now there is another one of those wiggle words, pussy words. You THINK you can? I don't like the word think. I don't think anything." V said not realizing the irony of what he was saying.

Lars did not dare point out that irony.

V continued. "Ragu said you CAN. And he put me in charge of managing you. People I manage don't think, they don't hope, they don't believe. They DO! Ragu said you CAN DO, and it is my job to ensure you fulfill that promise. Are we understanding each other, you little Nazi fuck!!"

All calmness and pretense of this being a polite conversation were now gone. Lars realized that he was now committed.

Fuck it, he thought, the Nazi's worked well with the Italians in World War II. He can deal with this muscle head for now. If things go south, he will give this grease ball a bullet between the eyes.

"We understand each other." Lars relented and then continued. "By the way, next time we meet, I will bring you a book about the Italian Socialist leader Benito Mussolini, I think it will change your opinion on my beliefs. They called him The Leader, or Il Duce."

"Yeah, you are going to need a douche to clean out your pussy if you keep talking smack, faggot. Now I think our little talk here is done. My associates and I will be visiting you and we will expect your game plan." V snapped indicating it was time for Lars to get the fuck out.

Lars stood up, clicked his heels and gave a very slight bow, doing his best to imitate the Nazi officers he had seen in movies. "Till then." he said, then stepped sideways out from between V and the chair and made his way to the door.

V watched his guest walk out the door of the cabin. "What the fuck?" he murmured to himself. He turned around, picked up the remote and turned on the TV to ESPN.

Ragu re-entered the room.

"Hey boss, I don't' get it. If you want that guy Ronan gone, I can put some of my guys on it. This why would you want to work with this little prick, he's worthless?"

Ragu positioned himself at a bar stool, which was a signal to V to walk over and pour him a drink.

"He's not worthless," Ragu replied. "Worth means having value, and the value of this little prick is whatever his worth is to others. It is all about wants and needs." Ragu was about to impart more wisdom. "Look at that poster up there." Ragu pointed to a black and white poster of Goodfellas which hand signed by the stars of the film. "That is just a piece of paper, with some ink. To some starving goat herder in Afghanistan, it is worthless. He can't eat it, he can't sell it, and he can't fuck it. Thus, its worthlessness. As for me, because I love that movie, it has value. That is why, when I saw it in the Sullivan's basement, I took it."

V pushed his lower lip up as if he were being educated by Socrates, while he handed Ragu a glass of Johnny Walker Blue.

Ragu continued. "Now let's look at our new President. He wanted to be a good and moral man. He also wanted to be in power. When he was a congressman, he had both morals and power. But then a funny thing happened. Now he has ascended to the top where he has real power, and he finds that he not only wants power, he needs it."

Ragu took a sip and continued. "As for morality," Ragu shrugged. "Patrick realized that while he WANTS it, he really does not NEED it."

Ragu got off the stool and moved over to the leather chair. "So now, let's return to the value of our little prick friend who just left. His life has a specific dollar value to someone close to our President. It's simple economics my large friend. Just like I took that poster; I will take his life."

CHAPTER 26:
Lars and the
Long Ride Home

Lars sat in the passenger seat of the black Mercedes as it was driven north. The car was acquired from a now deceased older gentleman who just couldn't wait for the contractors to declare the golf courses cleared and ready to re-open. The contractors had created zones throughout the state and were systematically clearing all Skells from each zone. Until a formal announcement of all clear, areas were considered no-go zones, meaning you ventured out on your own risk of death or arrest. No-go zones were unprotected and uncontained. Major medical, industrial and security areas were cleared first. Most all the college and university campuses, which had been serving as quarantine zones and holding pens for the infected in the beginning of the outbreak, were now cleared. These were then followed by residential neighborhoods and shopping centers. The golf course that the Mercedes owner frequented had not yet been cleared.

He had been on the fifth hole, a par 3, when he was attacked and eaten by Skells.

Jay and Lars were also taking advantage of the no-go zone to rob the golf course pro shop when they saw it all going down. After the Skells had finished their meal and wandered off, they scampered down to retrieve his keys from blood soaked polyester pants.

Lars contemplative silence upon leaving Ragu's hunting lodge went unnoticed by his driver Jay. Jay would never shut the fuck up. He was on constant transmit mode, and most of what he talked about was nothing. It was as if Lars was sitting next to a hurricane of words, just spinning endlessly. Stories, news, gossip and just general bullshit. You could not tell if Jay had something important to say, as he was saying so much, it was impossible to identify the signal from the noise.

If you asked Jay what time it was, he would tell you three o'clock. He would then tell you it felt later, like six o'clock. He would tell you why it felt later than it was. He would remind you when daylight savings time was beginning. He would remind you that this year's date was different from last year's date. He would tell you how stupid daylight savings time is. He would tell you about some time he was late for some such shit due to not setting his stupid watch to meet stupid daylights savings time. Jay was an avalanche of unwanted information.

Jay was rattling on about some story about he and his buddies back in high school. Another typical teenage war story of drinking beers in the woods and then being chased by cops. Most of Jay's stories involved cops chasing them through somewhere, the woods, the neighborhood, school. Those days were over a decade past, but for Jay, life was in stasis, and nothing much else of note had happened to him since those good old days.

When you peak in high school, you hang onto those memories for dear life.

"So, what were you doing in there?" Jay finally asked of his passenger.

Lars did not respond.

"Earth to Lars, yo, dude, you still with me?"

Lars shook his head slightly as if forcing himself out of a self-imposed trance. "What?"

"I asked what were you doing in there? That cabin used to be owned by some mob guys. We looking to align with them? The mafia? I would warn you against that. I have lived in this state my whole life. I don't know what the mob is like in California, but here in Jersey, it is the real deal. We used to sneak around the woods surrounding that place as kids, looking for bodies or guns and shit. Please don't tell me you borrowed money from them."

"I may have gotten myself into a bit of a business arrangement with them." Lars said meekly.

"Oh shit, man, that is dangerous territory, even for you. What is it?" Jay asked nervously.

"I...I met with Gary Ragu. I told him that I could take care of Ronan. Now, they want me to carry through with that boast. So, I would say yes, we are now a little bit involved with the mob."

"Lars!" Jay replied with panic. "Ragu's gang does not get a LITTLE bit involved with anything. That is like asking them to get your sister a LITTLE bit pregnant. They don't do LITTLE. They will fuck your sister big and hard, till both she and the girl next to her are pregnant. Oh, fuck man, this is bad."

"Chill the fuck out Jay, I have this under control." Lars said in a tone that seemed anything but in control.

"Can you do it?" Jay asked. "Can you assassinate Ronan? I am not against it, man. He is a real prick. He turned on the brotherhood. He cast us aside for some bitch. He deserves to die. But if you don't pull it off..."

Lars cut him off. "I can do it. I can get close to him and I can do it. He is not like Ragu or Callahan. He does not have security contractors or grease-ball thugs surrounding him. Ronan has only that Jew bitch of his, and she is the weak point. If I can find him, I can get close to him, and then I can kill him. Then we take over the brotherhood. No mixed signals. They will know I am in charge."

They drove for some time to get back up north, taking the side streets to avoid contractor checkpoints. They drove past PCRC deployed Kraken systems, some still emitting their hum, some vandalized or destroyed. They drove past white PCRC collection trucks, filled with Skells strapped in by the neck being transported to new, unknown Q-Zones. Some trucks were parked and their tan jumpsuit wearing PCRC contractor retrieval crews guiding their skin and bones, vicious, cargo up ramps via retractable poles.

They drove past neighborhoods bright and normal with kids playing in the streets, under the watchful eyes of their nervous parents, and through neighborhoods where not a living soul could be seen. As they got closer to Newark, they found streets that were still owned by Skells, with body parts from days old attacks still rotting on the sidewalk. They avoided no-go zone neighborhoods as best they could, as they were like driving through a living nightmare.

Lars wondered aloud if the rest of the country was in such a broken state.

Jay did not respond; he had been silent for over an hour.

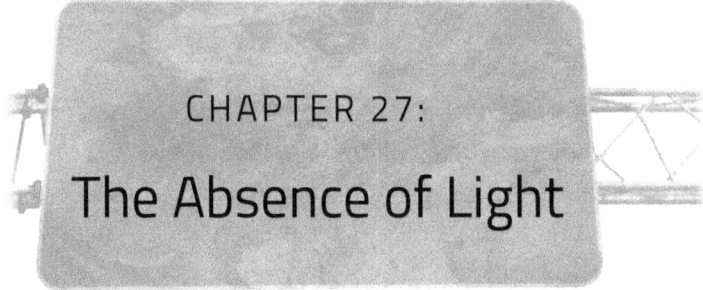

CHAPTER 27:

The Absence of Light

"What am I looking at here?"

"It is not what you are looking at, it's what is looking at you." Robert Kraus, CEO of Eye-Identify told Harry Rose and Daniel Sullivan.

"Cut the haiku, what the fuck am I looking at? A light, big deal, I am looking at a lighting fixture in the ceiling." Sullivan snapped.

"What you are looking at is the same lighting fixture that was there this morning. But it is not the same. We have turned out Eye-Identify. Our system does not need to change the existing legacy lighting system. You do not even need to upgrade to one of those curly cue halogen light bulbs. We work with the actual light that is emitted."

"Show me what the hell I am supposed to be seeing." Sullivan commanded.

He raised his iPhone and showed video of the tree men looking up at the light.

"Ok, so you have a camera up there. Big deal." Sullivan scoffed.

"No, that is the point. No camera. No new electronics at all. Our system, Eye-Identify, works with the actual light itself to broadcast high quality video. We are using the light to capture whatever it shines upon, to act as a video source, and feed information back via the WIFI and the power grid to connect with our main server. So, if you have a light that is connected to the power grid, that light can now serve as a camera, monitoring all it sees if it is on, day or night. We utilize WIFI to permeate the walls to pull in shapes and faces from rooms that are adjacent to a lighted room. The system, matched with our facial recognition technology, is the most powerful surveillance tool in the world."

"Wait, so you are saying, the light bulb itself is the camera?" Rose asked.

"Not so much the bulb, but the actual emission spectrum produced by the light serves as a source to capture and transmit image data. The light waves are absorbing the data that our system refigures into identifiable imagery. We plug this in to the grid, and it goes statewide. Anywhere there is a light bulb, a streetlight, shopping mall ceiling lights, or the night light in your kid's bedroom, if it is plugged in, it is transmitting video back to us. Which also means, if anyone you need to located is anywhere within the transmission of electric light, we can identify them to their exact location." Kraus replied with deep pride and satisfaction about his technology.

"This is insane, this is too much...too much...everything!" Rose finally spit out, unable to find more accurate words to describe his outrage. "This is invasion of privacy at a level not only unprecedented, it is unimagined!"

"Let's just wait a minute." Sullivan chimed in, trying to calm Rose. "You told me yourself that I needed to, and I quote, 'lock this shit down'. The situation is not getting better out there, in fact, it is getting a whole lot fucking worse. I will be honest with you, we are keeping most of the situation out of the press, but we have flare ups of infected popping up nearly every day now. It is a constant game of whack-a-mole. We need to make some bold moves to get the region to at least a state of somewhat normalcy. Whatever the definition is for normalcy in New Jersey."

"There is more." Kraus said. Are you familiar with A.I?"

"Artificial Intelligence?" Rose asked

"Close, but this is Anticipatory Intelligence. While the new Eye-Identify will track people in the physical world, we can now track them in the cyber world like never before. Even on the dark web. Our new scrapping tool scours social media, public, private and even TOR, to identify people and their cyber presence. We have been testing it for the past two years in the Middle East. The leaders there were not looking for another Arab Spring to catch them off guard. The combination of our Anticipatory Intel tools, synced with our facial recognition software and our Eye-Identify light sensor transmission is the perfect combination for when, let's say, a population is feeling a little too rambunctious and needs a time out."

Rose rubbed his eyes with his thumb and finger, trying to absorb this data.

"I can't imagine the President would allow this." he murmured.

"He already has approved it." Kraus responded. "Next week, he and Cardinal Remigio will be onsite for the official launch of The Center for the Management of Extraordinary Events. This agency will be a teaming of the best and the brightest technologists from government, academia and industry. We are very proud to have been asked to serve on the board."

"Let me guess, you are a subsidiary of PCRC?" Rose asked exasperated, but now putting the pieces together.

"Wholly owned, as of last week." Kraus replied.

Sullivan spoke up. "This is not a bad thing, Harry. We can't have vigilantes, sex traffickers, zombie merchants and neo-Nazi cyber terrorists running rampant. If we don't take care of this Ronan guy soon, he could very well be the next leader of the free world. At that point, invasion of privacy is going to seem like a day at Asbury Park. And this won't stop with Ronan, there will be another just like him when he is gone. And then another. We need the tools to manage this fight." Sullivan was not used to serving as the voice of reason. "Desperate times, man. Desperate times."

CHAPTER 28:

Citizens United

Majesty sat in the upscale, northern New Jersey restaurant. It was not a place she would ever visit on her own. The crowd appeared geriatric. Lots of thick steaks and thin fries being eaten by white men sipping martinis. It reminded her of the country club crowd her father was so beholden to. But she needed to fulfill her role as the future wife of the future president.

Gary had expressed a desire to help fund the campaign. He was a man of business that preferred to keep his political contributions discreet.

He had reached out to Majesty to express his desire to help Ronan, providing the new administration would not be interfering with Ragu's newfound dominance of Atlantic City.

She had sat there, watching the bald mobster and his giant associate wash down their filets with multiple glasses of scotch.

"So, as I was saying," Gary continued, slightly slurring his words. "I would like to make a sizable donation. And if you and your friend Mr. Ronan would like to accept my offer of friendship, I would of course be making this donation in cash."

"That is a lot of money to be handing over in cash." she suggested.

"I don't think a check is the best way to go, do you?" he countered with a mocking tone.

"Yes, yes, you're correct. So, where and when would we meet you to receive this donation," she asked.

"I think, for now, that we keep this between you and me." Ragu said, polishing off his fifth drink, his grin widening and his eyes zeroing in on Majesty's chest. "I don't know Ronan, but I feel I know you. I am sure I could get to know you better over time." he said. Little V chuckled.

She was disgusted at the overt sexism this man exuded. But she also felt it was best that she handled the money. She knew Ronan would not accept such a donation. He has no interest in money in general. It was one of the things she could never understand about the man. She, on the other hand, did understand the near erotic power that money possessed.

"Agreed," she said. "When do we make the transaction?"

"Hmm, the little lady is eager. I like that. I will have it delivered to a warehouse of mine. It is not far from here. Let's make this theatrical and clandestine. You will meet my deliveryman there at midnight tonight. You know him, he is an old friend of yours. Lars."

"You're kidding me. That asshole is working for you? I don't want to see him," she snapped.

"I'll tell you what, I understand you don't like him. I don't like him either, but as you know, blind dumb loyalty has its value. So how about I throw in an extra hundred grand. Just for you and for your inconvenience of having to deal with my current errand boy. That money will be our little secret. OK?" Ragu said getting up from the table with a bit of drunken difficulty.

Majesty looked at the yet to be paid bill still sitting in the leather folder the waitress had brought.

"Christ, I just gave this broad a hundred G's and this little Jewish princess still wants me to pick up the tab." Gary turned to his companion. "Hey V, look at me, I am the messiah, and I can answer the Jewish people's prayers!" Ragu threw a stack of bills onto the leather folder holding the dinner tab. "I am picking up the check. See. The Jews prayers are answered!"

With that, and the assistance of Little V, Gary Ragu stumbled toward the exit.

CHAPTER 29:

The Tick

At midnight, Majesty arrived at the address she was given. It was a salt and sand storage facility just off the garden state parkway. As she entered, she suspiciously scanned the room for threats. The structure inside consisted of a singular, open room. Other than the door she entered, there was only one other way in or out. Directly opposite the door was the loading dock, for trucks back into to receive their road salt or sand. Currently, the room was barren except for two folding chairs next to a small table.

She took a seat at one of the chairs to wait for the lecherous Mafioso. She was disgusted knowing she would have to be in his presence again. She felt equally hesitant about seeing Lars. She placed her handbag on the table, reached in and put her hand on her small 9mm weapon inside. An insurance policy just in case Lars was thinking about payback against her. She was here to collect the money and leave. She was done with men.

Majesty had come a long way from her not so humble beginnings. A child of wealth and privilege, well educated, she had found her calling while attending an elite university on the west coast. A near immersive indoctrination into the political left. But what most of the kids saw as an outlet to express this new-found rage; protesting, sit ins, chanting and the occasional sacking of the student store, she found this to be pointless and hollow. She wanted to change the country, change the world. She realized that while most of her fellow travelers seemed to wallow in their own empathy for the downtrodden. They were wracked with guilt at their own privileged birthright. She felt no such empathy. She felt no guilt, no remorse and no need to lift others up. She only felt the need to bring others down. She needed to even the score with those that had wronged her, who had tried to oppress her, who had offended her. And that list was long and growing by the day.

Lars once told her there were several lines of code missing from her mental programming. She saw that as a demonstration of her superiority. She was next generation. The body had long outgrown the need for molars, tonsils and appendix. Empathy and guilt were legacy appendages no longer needed in today's society. If only she could have had those traits extracted from Ronan's mental program, she and he could rule this planet. But Majesty knew she was special. She was ahead of evolution. But she understood in this sexist, patriarchal society, she needed Ronan's physical form to be the face of the movement. Her time would come to be anointed, to take the reins, and then, he, Ronan, and the rest of his male species, would be with her.

She saw a vehicles lights pulling up to the front of the building. The vehicle stopped and ceased its engine, yet the lights remained on, preventing her from seeing the face of the man entering the room.

As he closed the door behind him, she confirmed it was indeed Lars entering, but he was not carrying her cash.

"Ok, so, where is it?" Lars asked.

"Where is what?" she spat.

"The location. The address. The place I can go find Ronan?" he answered.

"What the hell are you talking about?" she snapped, "where is the money you are supposed to bring me?"

"Bullshit, you know the deal. Ragu told you he would give you the money after you provided us the location of Ronan. Where he would be alone, unarmed and I can go take care of him without trouble. Once that is done, you get paid." Lars explained.

"I have no idea what you are talking about. I am here to collect the money Ragu wanted to..." Majesty trailed off. She realized what was happening. They were both set up. She ran quickly to the only exit door and found it locked. She ran to the other side of the room and began yanking at the handle of the metal bay-door, but it too was sealed. She looked around for another way of escape. Lars stood in the center of the room, still clueless on what was occurring.

Majesty began pulling upwards at each of the four loading bay doors, but they would not budge. She ran around the nearly empty room searching for any type of weapon.

"Wanna tell me what the fuck is going on?" A rattled Lars shouted.

Majesty ran over and grabbed one of the folding chairs, she folded it up and held the two legs ready to swing at the first person was that was going to walk through that door.

Lars had not yet grasped the situation. Majesty was obviously not going to give him what he came for, so he turned his attention to the small air vent in the ceiling that was about eight feet above them.

"You lock the door?" Lars yelled at the ceiling.

"Hey, up there." Lars again began talking to the ceiling. "Can you see someone out there? Did someone lock the door"?"

"No, I am still on the roof." Jay whispered back, loud enough for both Lars and Majesty to hear. Jay had been positioned on the roof and was peering through the six-inch-wide air vent. Just wide enough to fit an arm through as well as the barrel of a rifle that he had planned to use to kill Majesty.

"You don't have to whisper; she knows you're there now." Lars commanded. "Just get down here and unlock the door."

They could hear Jay's body slide down the metallic roof off to the edge and then silence.

The ground beneath them began to vibrate as they heard a large vehicle approaching. There were no windows. But, Lars and Majesty tried to peek out of the sides of the bay door. It was the unmistakable sound of a large tractor-trailer. They could hear it circling the building, and then the repeating beeps from a truck backing up till it reached the bay doors. There were large metallic clanks as the back of the truck coupled and locked with the bay door.

Lars and Majesty were silent.

They heard sounds of Jay scurrying back up the roof like a 140lb squirrel. Still whispering, Jay informed them that it was a PCRC contractors truck but with Connecticut license plates. He also let them know that there were multiple armed contractors standing alongside the vehicle.

"What are they doing?" Lars asked, also in whisper.

"Hold on." Jay replied and they could hear him, slowly this time, sliding toward the edge. Minutes passed, and they could hear Lars shimmy back up.

They could see his face through the vent. Jay wore a broad maniacal smile on his face. He was giggling nervously.

"What?" Lars asked.

Jay started laughing.

"Why are you laughing? Keep quiet you idiot!" Majesty snapped, still holding the chair near the front door.

Jay kept trying to talk but his laughter is uncontrollably.

"Its...It's a tic." Jay said in-between gasps for breath.

Lars and Majesty looked at each other. Confused.

"It's a tic, I have had it since I was a kid," he said barely audible with laughter and gulps of breath; he was now bent over, his right hand holding himself up on the table, his left hand holding his stomach.

Lars couldn't help but to smile, followed by Majesty. Perhaps this was not a set up at all, but a comical misunderstanding.

"What the hell are you saying?" Lars asked, laughter breaking through his lips. He considered if they were the butt of a joke.

"It's...It's...when I get nervous...it's a tic I can't control." Jay spit out through bouts of high pitched freakish yet hysterical laughter.

The contagion had spread and Lars and Majesty were both now laughing audibly.

"It's a nervous tic, a reaction when I am scared or under stress." Jay sputtered, then took a deep breath to compose himself.

"You're dead!" he gasped, followed by an explosive laugh.

Through his own laughter, Lars was able to query "Whaaaat? What are you saying?" he asked, laughing between each world, he and Majesty exchanged looks, and slowly their laughter faded.

"No way out. You're...(laugh) so...(gasp for breath)...dead (spitting laughter)."

The laughter from Majesty ceased first followed by Lars.

"Uh, wait, what did you say?" Lars asked, his momentary laughter now extinguished.

"What the fuck are you saying you little prick?" Majesty yelled.

Jay's laughter was no longer funny. It was no longer infectious. It was no longer laughter. It was the panicked, involuntary spasms of a man who had lost all control. He took a deep breath and hoarsely screamed, "You're dead, we're completely surrounded, they're in the truck there are hundreds of them!"

The bay door flew open and crashed against the ceiling. Dozens of Skells fell into the room. They were being pushed out of the truck by a moving panel, pouring over one hundred ravaged bodies into the contained space.

Jay held down his arm from the small opening and Jay jumped up onto the small table and leaped for it like Tarzan swinging from a vine. He was successful and managed to grab hold of Jay's bicep with his right hand, and he pulled up his legs and steadied himself with his left hand. Beneath him, he saw Majesty attempting to fight off the flood by swinging her metal chair. By the second swing, she was enveloped and was being torn to shreds. He could hear Majesty shrieking beneath him and Jay shrieking in pain above him.

It took mere seconds for Skells to be packed into the room so tightly they could barely move. He saw an escape. The truck bay was now empty. If he could make it across the room and into the back of the truck--he had a chance.

High-pitched shrieks pierced the night as Jay howled in pain. Lars could feel Jay's bicep muscle separating from the bone. He swung his legs upwards, and could hear the sickening crack of Jay's shoulder muscle as it split in two. The arm gave way a bit more, allowing more loose flesh for Lars to grab hold of. He was ripping Jay in two in his attempts to hoist himself higher. At least, below him, the shrieking from Majesty had ceased, as her lungs had already been ripped out of her body. He heard a gurgled squeak escape her lips, and then she was no more.

Lars continued to focus on the truck bay. He had crowd surfed across the top of mosh-pits many times before. He figured out exactly what he needed to do. The Skells were packed shoulder to shoulder so tightly they could barely move or raise their arms above their heads. He curled his hands inside the sleeves of his leather jacket and lowered himself, boots first, onto their shoulders. As he released Jays arm, he heard a final moan from the man on the roof as the arm dangled through the vent, the limb now only attached to the body by skin.

Lars balanced himself on the shoulders for just a second, and then laid his body prone across their heads and shoulders, keeping his limbs high to avoid their gnashing teeth, and began shimmying towards the open bay.

Lars was swimming, literally swimming, on top of the infected. They could not even raise their arms up through the crowd to grab him or crane their necks into a position to bite him. He needed to keep moving. He saw light coming from the space at the exit bay. If he could just make it to that opening before the truck pulled out, he had a shot.

The snapping of hundreds of sets of teeth sounded like castanets. He slowly slid his body across their heads, he could feel their skulls through their tight skin. No meat, no tissue, just skin and veins and bone and clattering teeth behind curled thin lips. Their hair was falling off in patches, sticking to his sweating palms.

His feet were vulnerable but he trusted his steel toe Doc Martin boots to prevent any bites from penetrating through to his skin. He needed to keep his body prone, his fingers stretched out and to just keep sliding across the dead heads till he reached the space above the door.

The movement of the Skells shoving against one another reminded him of playing with parachutes when he was a kid. He could remember his time in second grade, when his classmates had encircled a multi-color parachute and were waiving it up and down. He remembered wanting to run underneath it to grab the toy. To run in, grab the toy and roll out before the parachute came down. He remembered his teacher Ms. Schwartz. He had loved her.

His hand slipped off a sweaty baldhead and his arm flung downward into the crowd. He pulled it up quickly.

From deep within the sea of Skells, a minnow leaped. A girl, about seven. He had not seen her deep in the crowd of blood soaked men and women, but she saw his hand, and she leaped into the air, right above the heads of the Skells, and she took the bait. Her teeth came clamping onto Lars middle finger. The minnow went back down into the crowd with his favorite finger clamped in between her teeth.

Lars's body followed his middle finger down into the angry sea of Skells. Just his Doc Martin's were left above the surface, bobbing up and down like two floating buoys in a sea. They undulated up and down, until finally, they too, sank into the ocean's depths.

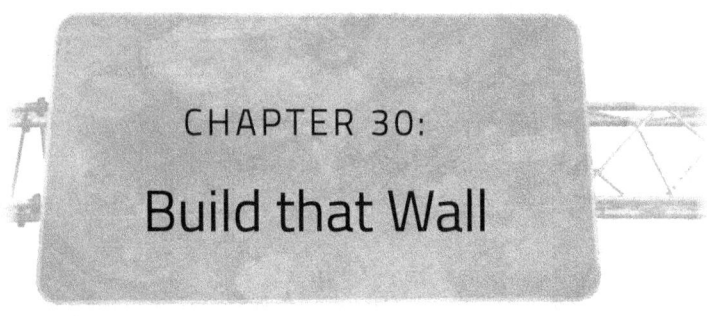

CHAPTER 30:

Build that Wall

Ronan began his nightly webcast on a somber note.

"Today, I must announce the sad and devastating loss of two of my inner circle. Majesty Steinman and Laurence 'Lars' Webber were both killed today. Killed by Skells. They were touring one of the quarantine zones and the safety procedures failed, and they were both horribly and brutally murdered.

"I do not blame the Skells, as they have no ability to understand their actions. They are merely another casualty of capitalist greed.

"It is my belief that they were murdered not by the Skells, but by powerful interests who wanted to hurt me. And hurt me they did. The Skells were merely the implements of death, no different than an illegally purchased assault rifle or a lead poisoned water system.

"But I will not expose my friend's killers, not today. To expose them would be to further hurt this country. I will weep for my friends. We will all weep for them. Then, we will move on. It is the country we must think of now.

"One thing is now certain. It is clear to me now that our President cannot keep us safe from the infected. So, I am stating today, that should you elect me as your new President, I will do what it takes to protect the nation from this threat. I will build a wall surrounding the state of New Jersey to ensure that the threat from Skells is contained.

"A wall that will ensure these murderous individuals do not spread and weaken our nation, as they have spread and weakened our beloved New Jersey.

I am also announcing my second platform. The Death with Dignity program. The infected cannot be saved, they cannot be cured and to keep them locked up is inhumane and dangerous. We must allow these people to be put to peace, for their sakes and for ours. Choose me as your leader, and this nightmare will be over, your children can sleep safe in their beds knowing there are no more monsters.

"There is only one choice America. We can continue under the failed containment policies of this administration, the lies of national Skell care, and the false hopes of a cure. Or we can grow together under my leadership. Let the G.R.A.SS movement grow America. Choose me as your leader. There is no other way forward."

CHAPTER 31:

Cloture

Daniel Sullivan rushed to greet his sister. When he heard that his brother James had taken Fiona off the Cape May White House grounds without additional security measures, he had been infuriated. He had already lost one sibling; he was not going to lose anymore.

He had a hug ready for her, and a left hook ready for his brother.

"Where is he?" Daniel asked, referring to his brother.

"He met a woman, an old girlfriend. He stayed back at the camp."

"Well, well, Brother James is scoring himself some post-apocalyptic pussy. Bout time." Daniel said, relishing the news of his brother's conquest.

"You know, I'm your sister, but I am still a lady, so why don't you hold the vulgarities. James stayed at back at the camp, as Colonel Tindall wants to turn himself in. He will turn himself over for arrest peacefully if you will allow his soldiers and the rest of his followers go their own way without any charges." Fiona informed the assembled White House staff that was arriving to greet her.

"Arrest him?" Daniel scoffed. "Shit, we want to promote him. First pardon him, or whatever it is you do with AWOL Colonels. Then we are going to make him a General. We need him here. Can you give me directions to this camp?"

Fiona deferred to Jack Jones who had accompanied her. "My friend Mr. Jones here will take you right now. He is a close adviser to the Colonel. I expect he too will be treated with the respect you will show the Colonel."

Woodrow came quickly walking down the hall and Fiona rushed to embrace him.

Daniel turned his attention away from the disgusting display to focus on retrieving Colonel Tindall. He followed Jack outside to the waiting Prius. Daniel stopped in his tracks.

"Shall I take you to the camp now?" Jack asked confused at the hesitation.

He gave Jack 'Smoothie' Jones the once-over.

"How about we take my car." Daniel replied as he pulled out his keys and remotely unlocked the black, heavily-fortified Escalade.

"Hey, this is nice, like I am getting picked up by an armored Uber." Jack quipped.

Daniel positioned himself behind the wheel and looked to his right as the entire vehicle rocked as Jack propelled his weight from the runner to seat himself in the passenger side.

"Try not to tip the vehicle over, ok fat ass" Daniel snapped.

As they began driving to Tindall's compound in the woods, Jack spoke up. "You know, I have never had a problem with my weight. Others have had a problem with it, but not me."

"Hey, I am not judging here." Daniel said. "I am just saying maybe you can pull the chair away from the buffet once and a while."

"You are an unhappy man, I can tell." Jack replied.

Daniel reached over and turned on the radio as if it could act as a muzzle.

Jack continued. "I spent years trying to find out why I was unhappy in my life. Was it because I was too fat, because I was in an unhappy marriage, or because I moved from one shit job to another? Then it occurred to me the underlying reason I was unhappy. I am just naturally an unhappy person. It was only after I realized I was an unhappy person that I stopped trying to find some sort of elusive happiness. So, from now on, I think I will just focus on making others happy. My wife and kids. Time to grow up and stop chasing some panacea that will make me happy and just focus on being a man. Being a husband and father. Perhaps it took the apocalypse to make things come into focus for me."

"This going to be a long drive?" Daniel asked exasperated.

"I can tell, you too are struggling. That is why you are busting my balls. Have you ever tried making others happy?"

"I make others dead." Sullivan growled.

"Woo, tough guy. You may need to pull over here, I am just so intimidated I can't decide if I am going to piss my pants or shit my shorts."

Daniel chuckled.

"There you go. I acknowledged that you're a tough guy. Did I make you happy?" Jack asked.

"You're an asshole." Was Daniels retort as he tried to hide his smile.

"Speaking of assholes, mine is ripe right now, I think I actually do have to change my shorts, living in the woods is not for people with my particular body type. Not the best bathrooms." Jack said, half joking.

Daniel let himself laugh. "Tell you what Mr. Jones. After we pick up the Colonel, you can come back to the White House with me. You can take a shower, get yourself cleaned up, and I will even give you one of our contractor uniforms to wear. Then I will have one of our vehicle drivers take you to your house. You should return to your wife and kids looking like the tough guy...I mean the MAN that you have become."

Daniel looked over at the smiling Jack.

"Sound like a plan Jack?"

"You can call me Smoothie." He replied.

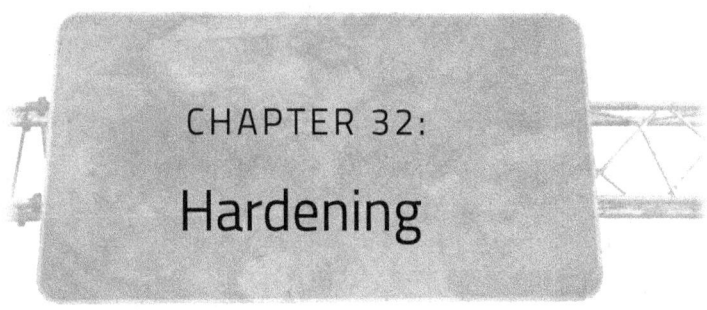

CHAPTER 32:

Hardening

"So, tell me about this cure." It was Tindall's first question to Harry Rose after turning in himself and his followers. As promised, they were not treated as fugitives, but as welcomed guests of the administration.

"On the drive to our new nation's capital," Tindall continued, waiving his hand referring to the Congress hotel they were currently residing in. "I was told that the administration has found a solution to the virus and that for some reason, I am to play an important part in curing the nation of what ails it."

Harry took a deep breath as he walked behind the desk and sat down uncomfortably in his chair. He looked down and shuffled some meaningless papers on his desk, avoiding Tindall's question for as many seconds as he could muster. He looked up and Tindall was still standing.

He held out his hand gesturing to the other chair for the Colonel to sit down.

"People are predictable in disaster; they are easy to manage. Disasters like this pandemic are not predictable. Like any influenza, it mutates as it moves from human to human. Highly pathogenic and virulent." Harry began.

"We would have to immunize 95 percent of the population to prevent continued epidemic outbreaks." Harry stopped speaking.

There was another moment of silence between the two men. Harry began to speak but did not know what to say. Tindall cut him off.

"You know, I spent four years of my military career in the Pentagon." Tindall began.

"I did not know that." Harry said, relieved that Tindall seemed to be changing the subject.

"My role there was as the program manager for a division that focused on military equipment survivability. Survivability involves the hardening of items to survive a chemical, radiological, or even electromagnetic pulse attack. We had to make decisions all the time on where we would invest our nation's tax dollars and where we wouldn't. I took the job very seriously as I was one of the few in government that considered our budgets to be just that; tax payer's dollars.

"Our choice was to put all equipment into one of two columns; either resiliency or redundancy.

"Large frame aircraft would fall into the resiliency column. If we spent fifty million dollars on an aircraft, it was worth spending the extra five million to ensure it could withstand the initial assault. Hardening meant the aircraft could be decontaminated should it be exposed to a chemical or radiological assault. We would refer to an aircraft that was toxic as being slimed, like in the Ghostbusters. If the aircraft got slimmed, we would have to decontaminate it. And then it could be quickly re-deployed to join the fight."

He continued, "But in the case of small ticket items, we would just focus on redundancy. Items in the redundancy column would include guns and uniforms, relatively low-cost items. They were plentiful, and if one were to be slimmed, we would simply throw it away and pull out another one from storage. Those items were disposable. If an item got slimmed, just dig a hole and bury it. Let the next generation worry about remediation."

Harry was listening intently but was waiting for the point.

"Over time, some high-ticket items that once warranted hardening became so plentiful and inexpensive to reproduce they shifted columns and became consumables, laptops being one of those items. I recall spending a small fortune on rugge-dized, hardened laptops back in the 90's. Laptops that could survive anything. We spent thousands of dollars per unit. But as time went by, those same laptops became less and less expensive. When a standard laptop could be purchased for less than five hundred dollars per unit, we realized that paying the extra expense of hardening them was pointless. If a laptop were to become damaged, we simply threw it away and replaced it with a new one from the manufacture. Usually the replacement was of better quality than the prior, upgraded or next generation as they say."

Harry nodded to show he was following and still waiting for the punch line.

"So, let me get to the point." Tindall said to the relief of his student. "How much would it cost to harden the public against this pandemic threat?" "How much to make each and every citizen of this country resilient against this virus? The cost of identifying, testing and administering a cure for all the infected and at the same time, researching, developing and mass producing a vaccine for the rest of the population?

"Tens of millions of dollars? Hundreds of millions? Millions of millions?

"The cost of resiliency would be too great of an expenditure, the more logical action is redundancy. Life is cheap. People are a disposable. The virus will burn itself out, like every other virus in human history. We will bury the dead, or in this case, the slimmed, and move on. Have I got the picture?"

"A final decision has not been made. This is still a policy in discussion." Harry replied sheepishly.

"I am sure it is. These decisions take time. Let me take a shot at some of the more salient points. What percentage of the country is infected right now? If a sizable percentage of our population died, what are the alternatives? Going to be expensive to re-populate. Perhaps bring in cheaper, more efficient citizens from Mexico or China? I am sure China would not mind sharing a couple millions of their own. Though I am sure the agreements struck would be the same as Chinese Pandas coming to U.S. zoos. The Chinese government would loan us the people, yet have right of return on all offspring. Might be worth thinking about. The Chinese models work harder, consume less, and require less ongoing maintenance and healthcare. Much more efficient than the typical American made citizen. Let's not forget, they are more, shall we say, accepting, of living under an un-elected ruling class.

"Perhaps we import the South American models. They too are very hard working and great for re-population, and most likely their respective nations would not require the return of offspring. Either option has its pros and cons. I doubt we could import from Europe. The EU has the lowest birth rates around, so they are having their own production problems to deal with. Last option would be to import from the Middle East and Africa, but sure that baby was killed in the crib. Do I have an accurate snapshot of where the administration currently stands?"

"The administration has no formal position. As I said, it is being reviewed."

"Meaning the President does not know that the decision has been made, he thinks that there still is a chance for some sort of positive outcome of this mess, correct?" Tindall pressed.

Harry leaned forward in his chair towards Tindall. "And for now, we will keep it that way. The President has a lot on his shoulders right now, we don't need him to bear the weight of hypotheticals. We are studying all options, and there is a chance that these choices will never need to be made and the situation will resolve itself, without need for imports. I am hoping you are the man to help us make that happen. Can I count on you?"

Tindall stood.

"You have my full support. Now, let me inspect my troops."

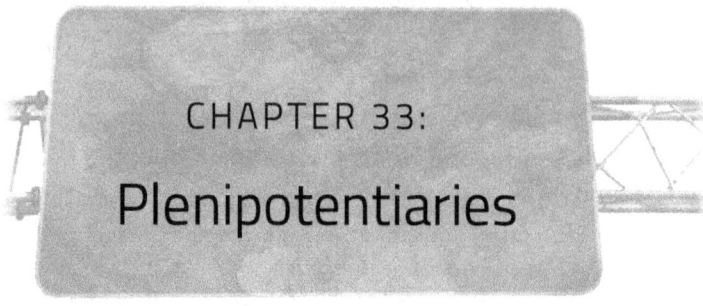

CHAPTER 33:

Plenipotentiaries

Colonel Tindall paced in front of the new VINNI recruits.

"My name is Colonel James Tindall, and I will be leading this new program. You people are all here because you are exceptional."

The men and women were standing together in the large storage area. They ranged in age from early twenties to some appearing to be in their late sixties. All were thin and wearing freshly provided light blue tactical outfits, each with five-digit number embroidered onto the right chest pocket.

"Some of you in this room know me. You came with me from my camp. But a great many more of you are meeting me for the first time. I understand what you are thinking. You are feeling anxious, scared, and perhaps even angry. You don't know why the administration brought you here, what plans they have for you. I want to assure you, they have been keeping you here not as prisoners, but for your own safety.

"You know, and we know, that you are different. I am sure that the physical change what has taken place since your exposure to the virus hasn't been subtle. Perhaps when family, friends, coworkers saw your radically altered appearance, they were a little more than suspicious. Some may have reacted negatively towards you, displayed fear of you, or perhaps even reacted violently towards you. I know some of you, not all, but some, may have committed acts that were beyond your control since the exposure. Acts you feel ashamed of or assume you will be facing punishment for.

"I want you to know that I understand, and that there will be no investigations, charges or trials under my watch.

"But, not everyone is as open minded and understanding as I am. Before we introduce you to the world, we need to better understand what your place is in the evolutionary hierarchy.

"Since your infection and transformation, you are different. What's truly disconcerting is that your difference is not easily identifiable. It's subtle and can even be alluring.

"Mankind will see your difference as dangerous, and will want to understand how you fit in this world. They will also want to know how we, the uninfected, original flavor humans are going to fit alongside you.

"When there are more of you, and there will undoubtedly be more of you, how will you view us?

"Are you simply an anomaly, or the next steps in human evolution?

"I am not going to lie to you, in some ways, your condition has made you superior to the rest of us. And as humans, we have always been on top of the food chain. I don't think people will take too kindly to be becoming second tier.

"I am sure most all of you will you will want to pursue your normal lives. Will want to walk into the future besides us. Others may look at you as being beneath them, which will be unpleasant for you. Others will look at you as threats, as terrorists, as dangerous, as ticking time bombs that need to be registered and monitored. Some will cower while they see you as the first step towards the extinction of the rest of us. Unfortunately, all of them may be correct. We just don't know what you people are yet."

Colonel Tindall looked down at his clipboard. Without looking up, he read out the name of one of the people on that sheet in front of him.

"David Donahue, please step forward."

A lean man in his late twenties made his way nervously to the front of the room.

"David?" Colonel asked.

He nodded.

"Big Dave Donahue. Big Dave, Double D, also known as Donut Destroyer." Tindall read the man's multiple aliases from the file.

Big D took a deep breath.

"Sir, I read your bio, your dossier so to speak, and man, the way you got here is ironic." Tindall commented with a slight chuckle. "Attacked at MacDonald's. Slowed down by fast food. Since one of the Skells took a bite out of you right there at the food counter, would that make you fast food or slow food?"

Tindall raised his eyes from the pages to view the silent, unamused David.

"That is a paradox, I tell you what." Tindall continued. "Mr. Double D, I am happy to have you here, but do me a favor. No more blogging about using Skells to lose weight. It is just too enticing and I am afraid a lot of people won't be as lucky as you, and will end up either dead or Skell-bound. We understand each other?"

David nodded, again, "Yes Sir."

Colonel Tindall looked over at another one of his recruits. "You, they guy missing his finger, what's your name?"

The man was taken by surprise and nervously began to answer. "Virg...um uh. Victor."

"Ok, Virg-uh-Victor. I will be honest with you. I don't care what your name is. As to me, you are all VINNI's." Tindall turned his attention to another. "You, young man," he pointed at a thin man in his twenties. "What is your name?'

The man thought for a moment. "Vinny?" he asked and answered all at once.

"Don't be a smart ass. I mean your real first name." Tindall replied.

"Scott Vanderst..."

Tindall cut him off before he could finish his sir name. "Didn't ask you for your life's story son, just your first name."

"Miss, what is your name?" Tindall barked at a woman in the front.

"Virginia sir," she answered.

"Well that makes it easy, I know what state I am sending you to. But you don't need to call me Sir. From this moment forward, you may call me James. No Sir. No Colonel. Just James. And let me be clear. I don't care what you have done, who you were, or who you ate. Your life starts over today. Most of you will never be accepted back into your old lives. What is important is you know who you are now, and you move forward. Is that understood?"

Some nods and yeses followed haphazardly.

"I said, is that understood!?"

"Yes Sir!" they all said loudly.

"What did I say to you about what to call me?"

"Yes James!" they shouted, several now smiling.

A middle-aged man raised his hand and was acknowledged by Tindall. "Yes, you there, the VINNI in the back."

"Um, James, can you tell us what our role is in this new mission? Do they intend to turn us into soldiers?"

"Soldiers, no sir, this is a new country. A divided and frightened country. And we need your assistance. Our President is counting on you to serve as ambassadors to his administration. Community organizers if you will. During elections, you will be poll watchers. You will be sent across this country, to major population areas and rural towns. You will serve as the face of this administration. You will be community organizers. You will be poll watchers at the upcoming elections. You will be diplomats. But instead of representing America in foreign lands, you will be representing both the administration and New Jersey to the rest of the country.

"We're not freaks!" an angry voice from the back called out.

"Excuse me?" The Colonel asked annoyed at the interruption.

An older man with glasses stepped to the front of the room. "I said we are not freaks."

"Sir, I do not believe I used that term. Nor do I think that of you. I do not believe I have spoken to you in a manor other than that of civility and professionalism."

"You don't have to say it; you are thinking it. They all are."

"Sir, please don't attempt to postulate that you have any idea what I am thinking. Your kind may have some semblance of a brain growing in your stomach, but unless that brain has mastered mind reading, you are simply making conjecture."

"All we are is what's next. We are the new." The old man spoke up with confidence in his voice. "There is always someone one new or something new to replace what is old. And the *new* always threatens the *old*.

"I would know. I was the old. I installed landline phones for a living. I saw the end of my career coming when I saw what was new, what was next. The 'next' made landlines, and the people who installed them, irrelevant. Next came fiber optics and I was bumped to second fiddle. Soon I was call in just to install the occasional fax machine. Then even the fiber guys were not needed as everything went wireless. Landlines and fax machines became as useless as VHS machines and the people who repaired them. Well, now, for the first time in my life, I am what's 'next'. I am no longer irrelevant. The old, the irrelevant, with all due respect sir, are people like you."

Tindall paused. "That may be true sir. But I hope, at least for a time, we all, even with our differences, can live together. Peacefully and with respect of each other's differences."

The man stepped back into the crowd.

"Tonight," Tindall began his summation. "The President of the United States, OUR President of OUR United States, will address the nation. He announces that in forty-eight hours, the country will hold a special election. The citizens will choose if he should continue as the leader, or if the country would like to turn itself over to the likes of Ronan. I am sending you out across this great land of ours as poll watchers. You will not be associated with this administration; you will be independent. But you will ensure the sanctity of the voting process. You will ensure the country chooses what's next."

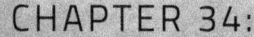

CHAPTER 34:

State of the Union

"My fellow citizens." Patrick began his broadcast.

"My name is Patrick Callahan and I am your President. I apologize that it has taken me so long to address the nation, but as you know, we have had a lot on our plate these past several weeks.

"I am broadcasting to you live via TV, radio and internet stream from my desk in the temporary oval office, which is located within the temporary White House here in Cape May, New Jersey.

"Rest assured, my resolve to rid this nation of the virus and to serve as your President is not temporary.

"I know you have all been troubled by the recent pronouncements form the terrorist Ronan and his criminal organization called G.R.A.SS. Yes, I called him a terrorist. He is also a criminal, a murder and a liar. I do not use these terms as hyperbole.

"That is why he remains as elusive as his promises. He uses social media to communicate Twitter, YouTube, Facebook and all the other social outlets that enable his hate speech while providing him his anonymity.

"Since the founding of this nation, there have been those that sought to divide us as a people. They may come from the left or the right, but their goal is clear. It is to divide and conquer.

"They hurl insults and throw around terms they don't even understand; fascism and communism, voter fraud and voter suppression, global warming and cultural rotting, war on women and war on Christmas.

"They make these claims and their most rabid believers follow them blindly, repeating the words like parrots. These zealots offer no proof of their accusations, even science and faith are politicized.

"Their accusations are everywhere, institutionalized, yet invisible. We can't see it, we can't touch it, yet they ask that we just accept it is there. Like oxygen, or nuclear fallout.

And that is why I have tried to take us in a new direction.

"Because there is something else all around us, something untouchable, unknowable."

"Yeah, it's called bullshit." Daniel said as he sat down on the office couch next to Harry. He handed him a beer and tossed another to BMW who had found a comfortable leather chair near the window. Daniel popped open his own can and continued to listen to his boss's broadcast.

"This invisible force is more dangerous than any of the 'ism's', cooling's, or wars our political enemies have thrown at us.

"It is more alluring, more attractive, more devious and insidious than any enemy we have faced before.

"It is the devil!"

Daniel spit out a mouthful of beer with such force that the liquid splattered TV screen.

"The devil is here, and it is all around us."

"Holy fucking shit, what hell did he just say?" Daniel yelled. "Is he talking about the devil, like the Jersey Devil? Or the red guy with horns? Is this really being broadcast!?'

Harry sat stunned and motionless.

Patrick continued his sermon about God and Satan.

"Holy fuck," BMW said to Sullivan. "It seems Patrick was the only one of us who paid attention in Sister Pugs religion class."

"These aren't his words." Harry spoke up. "These are being fed to him by our Vatican guest. The President is exhausted. He is mentally and emotionally drained. This exorcist asshole has gotten into his head and we let him. The next time Callahan is separated from this guy, I want you two to provide our holy friend a lift to the airport. The sooner, he is back on his way to Rome, the sooner we can clean up this mess."

Patrick finished his holy rant and returned to the subject of G.R.A.SS. Harry raised his hand to silence the room, as this was a topic he wanted to hear.

"This is not a time to merely condemn the deplorable actions of this terrorist group. Today, I am declaring the illegality of the organization called G.R.A.SS stating that it is an enemy of the United States and thus the group, their ideology and their members are to be eliminated."

"He is going to unify the country by starting a war?" BMW asked.

"No," Harry responded. "He is going to unify the country by winning a war."

CHAPTER 35

Post Convention Bounce

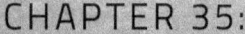
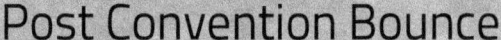

Patrick's first presidential address to the nation was over. Normally, there would be a walk out of the chamber to the thunderous applause of the congress and senate. There would be politicians who loved him and hated him scrambling to get close to him and shake his hand as he walked down the aisle. Then they would run to the waiting cameras, the spin room as it was referred to, where they would praise, or ridicule, to whatever it was the president had just said. But that was then, this is now.

The hallway was filled with paid contractors and stunned bureaucrats and functionaries.

There were two familiar faces in the crowd.

Patrick walked through the hallway, flanked by Harry, 9104 with Daniel Sullivan following closely behind.

"Mr. President!" the familiar voice called out. Patrick recognized the voice and turned around, seeing Ivan and Marifi being held back behind a wall of contractors.

"Mr. President!" Ivan called again. "It's me, Ivan. May I have a word?"

"Christ," Patrick said, "If today was not bad enough. Tell him another time."

Harry leaned in, "um sir, it might be best to bring him in. We have been looking for him and if he wants to come, would make things simple."

Patrick looked at Harry with indignation. "Really, you need me to help you do your fucking job? Fine, have him come along."

Harry motioned to the contractors to let Ivan through. They made a space for him, but did not allow Marifi through, not realizing they were together.

"Ivan!" she yelled after him but he did not stop or turn, his fixed his eyes on the back of Patrick Callahan.

"Ivan!" she yelled again, realizing that he must hear her. It was then that she noticed his hand reaching into his pocket.

Ivan had synced up with the flow of the crowd following the President.

"Ivan!" she called again. She saw him reaching into his back pocket.

As Ivan quickened his pace, to catch up with Daniel. He was within arm's reach of the President.

"Wait! Ivan!" she called again as she struggled with two contractors who were becoming more forceful in their restraint of her.

She could see Ivan's hand slide slowly out of his back pocket, and caught a glimpse of the silver blade from the palm sized Tanto point knife he now held.

Ivan was now parallel with Daniel and they exchanged looks. Ivan smiled and Daniel gave Ivan a 'Can you believe this shit?' head shake.

Ivan was now inches from Patrick's spine. Patrick removed his jacket and tie as he walked, tossing them towards an aide. Ivan had noticed the man looking gaunt and stressed on television, but up close, it was striking to see the physical toll recent events had taken on the man.

The crowd continued its flow down the hallway; Patrick was surrounded, yet in alone in his own world.

His wife and kids had abandoned him. Not really "his" kids, he thought. They are her kids. Hers and her ex-husbands. He had taken them on as his own, and now they were off on an island hiding. Cowering and providing him no support in his darkest hour. He had taken on the citizens of this nation as his own. He accepted them just as he had accepted his own bastard stepchildren. And they all had turned their backs on him. His dark thoughts metastasized.

He did not run for this office. He did not want this job. This supposed honor. This burden.

He was no different than some pathetic Hollywood assistant, whose job it was to hold the nations hair back while it puked into the gutter. A once great actor who was now a drugged-out train wreck, ending their career with a public spiral, desperately re-tweeting other people's creativity all while sinking into irrelevance.

They say some men were born great and others had greatness thrust upon them. He felt he did not fall into either of those buckets. He had taken command of this ship, and he deserved to stay in command. This public mutiny led by some cyber scumbag who can murder people, but save a tree, and thus is loved by the media. They listen to emotions and intentions, but don't want any real actions. He will give them action. He will take this country in the course it needs to go, and they will come alone and be the obedient citizenry.

Max was right. The Contractor program will be expanded, will protect this nation from itself. The MEAT program will expand, but this time it will be done correctly. The Skells and the VINNI's, they will...

Patrick stopped in his tracks, grabbing his side and letting out a loud yelp. His body contorted as if he were feeling stabbing pains in his back and side and chest all at once.

Ivan. No! Marifi could be heard shrieking from down the hallway.

Patrick slammed to the ground hard gasping for breath. 7322 was the first to his side. Daniel Sullivan pushed Ivan aside as he too dove to the ground next to Patrick and the contractors formed a secure circle. A woman screamed. The Presidential Physician came running from the back of the group and quickly got to his knees next to a gasping Patrick.

"He's having a heart attack!" The doctor yelled.

Ivan, who had frozen in his tracks, returned the clean, unused knife to his pocket.

The doctor ripped open Patrick's shirt and began resuscitation.

"Get him to his office couch, get these people out of here!" 7322 yelled.

Three contractors picked up the president and carried him down the hallway and around the corner out of Daniels sight.

Daniel grabbed two contractors "You two, clear this building, do not say anything to anyone, don't tell them what is happening, just clear this building now and make sure no fucking press are lurking to take pictures or video. This didn't happen, understand!?"

Daniel checked his gun. "Ivan, you need to get the fuck out, you don't know who is..." As he looked up from his weapon, he realized he was talking to himself.

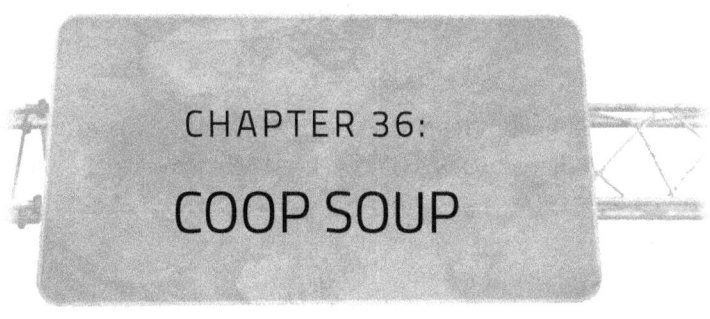

CHAPTER 36:

COOP SOUP

The door of the president's office burst open and Sullivan and Rose laid Patrick on the couch.

"He is unconscious but I think he is still alive." Rose said taking the Presidents pulse.

Harry Rose got up, opened the door to the hallway and shouted to the Contractors. "Don't let anyone into this office!" He closed and locked the door.

"Jesus Christ, this is bad." Harry said as he walked across the room and collapsed into Patrick's chair rubbing his forehead with his palm.

"Your ass getting used to that seat already?" Sullivan commented.

Harry looked down, just then noticing the significance of the chair he chose to plop down in. "Shut the fuck up Sullivan, I'm not in the mood."

An interior door leading from the Presidents private quarters into his office opened. "What the hell is going on?" Said the voice. Max Gold entered the room followed by the contractor Bankowski. "What's happening to him?"

"He had a heart attack." Rose replied.

"Well why the hell is he here, why is he not in the hospital? Max demanded

"Are you kidding me? This Ronan cocksucker is already ahead in the polls. All we need is the public knowing our president is having heart troubles. The nation will vote that psychopath in and we will be executed." Daniel snapped back.

"I was told you had Ivan. He is here, where the hell is he?" Max barked back to Daniel.

"He's gone." Daniel Sullivan replied, and then fiddled with his earpiece as if someone were talking to him.

"Gone? What the fuck do you mean gone!?" Max was infuriated.

Daniel waived him off, distracted by his earpiece. "Yeah, let him in." Daniel said into his mic and turned to Max. "What do you not understand about gone. He left. I don't know where he went, I was dealing with this shit!" he said with a hand wave to the prone president.

BMW was granted access to the room.

"Holy shit," he said upon first spotting an unconscious Patrick.

"Yeah, that seems to be the phrase of the day." Daniel replied.

Max turned to Bankowski "Get on line, I want every CCTV activated and I want Ivan's face tracked by the recognition program. I want you to find him now!"

"He's good as found." the oaf replied and left the room.

"Ok Sullivan, BMW, you two played football together." Rose said, snapping back into leadership role. "We need to quarterback this thing. We need a plan to either get him to a secure medical facility or have one brought here. And we need a cover story. If anyone can spin some bullshit, it's you."

Bankowski returned to the room and motioned to Max "I told you it was quick, we just caught him on the parkway camera. He is about to enter the bridge over Egg Harbor."

"Shut it down. Shut that bridge down and trap him on it!" Max ordered.

"Sir, I have a half dozen fully loaded meat wagons on either side of the bridge." Bankowski said, referring to Skell collection vans as the meat wagons. "I have directed them to stop traffic and dump their contents onto the road. That bridge is about to become a buffet."

"Not good enough, I want to be sure. Is that bridge rigged? If so, take out the full bridge." Max said.

"Um, Sir, that will be pretty fucking noticeable. A Skell attack we can explain. Shit, it's happening nearly every day. But we blow up the fucking bridge, I think people are going to start asking questions." Bankowski demonstrated a rare moment of "if this than that" reasoning.

Max leaned into Bankowski' s face. "If they ask questions, you tell them to shut the fuck up. If they don't shut the fuck up, you rip their tongues out. Is that understood? I said...blow that fucking bridge!"

BMW did not look over towards the two colluding men, but he heard every word. "I am going to find some medical supplies." BMW announced. He left the room and made his way towards the helicopter-landing pad. He did not know what the two were up to, but they wanted Ivan dead. Wanted it bad enough that they were going to kill an entire bridge full of commuters to ensure the job was done. He needed to get there first and see if there was any way to stop what was going to happen.

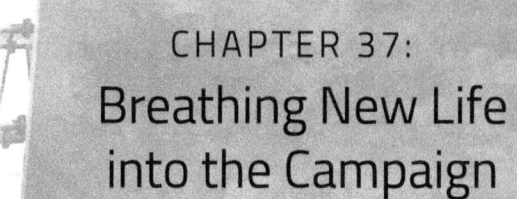

CHAPTER 37:
Breathing New Life into the Campaign

Woodrow and Fiona rushed into the President's office.
"Jesus Christ!" he yelped as he ran over to kneel beside Patrick.

"Get away from him you fucking quack, he doesn't need a witch doctor." Max snapped.

Woodrow ignored the insult and began attempts to resuscitate. "We need to get him to a hospital!"

"We can't, the public see's us carting his body away on a stretcher, and then he will lose the election. We need to keep this quite for another 24 hours."

Woodrow had risen to his feet. "There is another way. I have an idea but I can't guarantee it'll work." He turned to the contractor that escorted him. "Please go get Fiona and ask her to bring up our two friends."

The contractor nodded and left.

Woodrow post took a breath. "I want you to hear me out completely before you react.

"Patrick was the initial source of this virus correct? I mean his DNA was the one that was given to the scientists to develop the initial strain. Am I correct?"

Everyone in the room turned and looked at Max who took a step back from the sudden attention.

"Yes." he said, not realizing the word had audibly left his lips. "Yes." he said again, more forcefully, begrudgingly admitting what everyone already knew.

"Okay." Woodrow continued.

"I have experimented on the two types infected. The ones we call Skells, which look like walking corpses and VINNI's, the ones that look like long distance runners.

"Skells are beyond saving once the infection has fully taken hold. Their brains have melted away and the replacement brains that have grown in their stomachs have no more consciousness than the ability to drive these creatures to hunt and feed. They are without thought or reason.

"But the VINNI's are very different. They have been infected with the identical virus, and the initial symptoms are similar, the absorption and burning off all excess body fat, the increased aggressiveness, the insatiable hunger. But their virus shuts down faster, before the effects are too damaging.

"Their physical appearance is drastically changed, but to them, for the better. There seems to be no change to the internal organs. Their brain is intact, but slightly...reshaped. It is very subtle.

"They can be just like you and me. They can work, they can live, and they can love. They seem to have almost no desire, or need, to eat. But while their appetite has waned, their libido has been increased. They go through periods with insatiable desire to mate. Upon completion of the act, they go into a trance-like state and devour their partner.

"When not in that state the VINNI's are still their pre-infection selves."

Woodrow spoke up. "I have been running some tests on VINNI's. They are much healthier than they where prior to infection. What I'm looking to do is synthesize VINNI blood and give it to Patrick to save his life."

"What? Are you kidding me! You going to turn him into one of these fucking zombies!?" Daniel said.

"No, I don't feel that it will affect Patrick the way it affected the others, but I do feel it will save his life. It's my belief that since it was his DNA that created this virus, I feel Patrick could get all the benefits without the side effects. He is already skin and bone, so there is going to be very little visible change to his appearance."

"This is insane!" Patrick's doctor spouted. "Who is this man?"

7322 looked over at Daniel and nodded.

"Ok, everyone out of the room now!" Daniel commanded.

The doctor stood up. "I am not leaving. The President is my patient and he's dying he may only have a minute left."

Daniel raised his weapon. "That's why you better get your ass out of here in 30 seconds."

The doctor huffed and walked out of the room.

Fiona prepared a needle and injected Patrick with a serum.

The prone President took a breath and then laid still, his breathing shallow but steady

"How long does it take?"

"Take to what?"

"I have no idea I haven't done trials."

"So basically, the President of the United States is patient zero?"

"Well for a lack of a better word, yes."

BMW looked around the room, "Hey man you think we better get some like non-disclosure agreements signed between us?"

CHAPTER 38:

Bridge-Gate

On the bridge, Ivan soon realized that this particular traffic jam was not the naturally occurring phenomenon commuters must deal with in New Jersey. The bridge had been blocked, purposefully, and he was confident that he and Marifi were the cause. They had been spotted. He and Marifi exited their car and began running to the opposite end. It was then he saw them. Two white PCRC containment trucks behind him, both with cargo bay doors open and Skells pouring out. No doubt about it now, they were the target. They had to get off the bridge, but chances were, more trucks were arriving at the opposite end as well, pouring out more flesh hungry creatures. They were going to kill every poor sap that was stuck on this bridge just to ensure they got to him. He looked upwards and there he saw them. Traffic cameras. How could he have been so fucking stupid?

More people began fleeing their cars and running. He pointed to a large group that had formed and was moving towards the walkway. He indicated to Marifi they should blend into the crowd. Behind them, the Skells had begun finding their prey, and screams mixed with the blaring car horns.

Two people ran past them in the other direction. Then more, one man slamming into Marifi, knocking her over and sending her golok sword skidding across the ground underneath a van. She began crawling on her belly to retrieve it when a woman stepped on her back and another tripped over her prone body and hit the ground face first. The quantity of people running from the other direction indicated the other Skell delivery trucks had released their vicious cargo on the opposite end. There was no way off this bridge Ivan thought, that was when he realized Marifi was no longer buy his side.

He yelled out to her, spinning from side to side, when he caught glimpse of her legs disappearing underneath a van. "We need to go up, not down!" he yelled pointing to the scaffolding. He pushed his way towards her but now the steady stream of people running in both directions knocked him around like a pinball. He fought his way to the van just as he saw his first Skell. It was a man. He thought it was a man. The figure was ravaged and soaked with blood from head to foot. Their eyes met and the creature began to lunge at Ivan, but before it could get footing, it was hit from behind with the force of a linebacker by a large man fighting off two attackers. The man grabbed a handful of hair from a naked female Skell and with a couple back and forth yanks, ripped her head off her body. This appendage only served as a repository for the teeth, as the hands and body still wrestled the man, as the second male Skell continued to rip chunks of flesh from the man's large midsection.

Ivan pulled his eyes away from this spectacle and threw himself to the ground, finding Marifi, thankfully still there, gripping her sword. They lay on their stomachs, looking at each other, searching for those final words.

CHAPTER 39:
Peaceful Transition
of Power

Bankowsi returned from retrieving his laptop. He placed it on the now stricken president's desk and began typing.

Max came over and sat in the Presidents now vacant chair. He leaned over to get a closer look at the screen that was displaying CCTV cameras from the bridge. Chaos had erupted as the infected filed out of the containment trucks parked on either side of the bridge and began feeding, as if they were a herd of goats dropped off to eat their way through an overgrown grass field.

"Where is he!?" Max snapped searching the screen for Ivan.

"He was hiding under that van with the woman." Bankowsi informed. "Should I blow the bridge?"

"No, not yet, I have to be sure he is there. Can you get some of your men out there?" "Are you kidding me, they would not last a minute. That bridge is a death trap right now, we need to blow it before those creatures start overrunning the barricades and get off the bridge."

"Wait, look!" Max shouted as he pointed to the screen. He could see Ivan and Marifi snaking out from under the van on their stomachs. They each waited till the other was clear and began running to the side of the bridge.

"There, there they are. Go for it, blow the bridge now!" Max yelled, causing Daniel to take notice.

Bankowski began to type, but then looked closely at the screen.

"Hey dipshit," Sullivan said to Bankowski. "You actually took your fingers out of your ass long enough to learn to type? Guess you will need someone else to manipulate your prostate."

Bankowski stood up ready for a fight. "Shut the fuck up Sullivan!"

"Both of you idiots shut up!" Max yelled and pushed Bankowski back down to his knees to continue working the laptop.

Bankowski bristled but then returned his attention to the screen. He stopped and looked closer.

"What? What is it?" Max asked.

Bankowski used the mouse to open another window, one that was displaying a different CCTV camera. He panned the camera in the direction that Ivan and Marifi were running. In the sky, just off the bridge, a helicopter was hovering.

"What the fuck?" Both Max and Bankowski said in unison as they both looked up and scanned the room realizing BMW was gone.

"That mother fucker!" Bankowski yelled.

"Blow it now!" Max yelled.

Bankowski typed in three numbers and hit enter. He did it again and then again, each time pounding harder as if the force of the keypunch was what was causing the bridge not to blow.

"It's not working, I...I don't have control of the system? I can't even switch cameras; the system is frozen."

"Well do something, reboot, get to another computer." Max demanded as Bankowski slammed his fist on the table and left the room to find another laptop. Max watched the live camera feed as the video continued to steam.

He watched as the helicopter flew closer to the center of the bridge. He saw Ivan and Marifi fighting their way through the crowds.

BMW tracked Ivan and Marifi as they traversed the apocalyptic scene on the bridge. Cars had tried to demolition derby their way through the parking lot, smashing into each other, only making the path more impassible. Some cars had burst into flames, trapping those unfortunates to stay put and be burned alive, or flee and be eaten.

A chorus of screams rose from the bridge, loud enough that Malcolm could hear them even over the sound of the copter blades. He knew it was a futile attempt to save the doomed but he thought if he at least tried to find a location to put down or even get low enough to get the two on board, it was worth the risk. A few Skells had peeled off the easier prey of bridge victims and were chasing after Ivan and his wife. BMW could see Ivan was struggling to keep up and frequently slowed to a walk to catch his breath. Marifi would stop and wait while he waived her to keep moving forward. She disobeyed.

BMW saw a tractor-trailer that had flipped onto side about 100 yards ahead. He positioned the helicopter over the sideways vehicles and hovered, signaling to the couple a possible safe place to get high enough that he to escape the growing number of pursuers chasing them.

He saw Ivan point to the holding pattern and again, the couple began hoofing it in that direction.

BMW kept his attention on them too long, and did not realize the welcome party coming down the road from the opposite direction.

Before he could determine the best path to alert them that the area was no longer safe, they were approaching where the truck lay, unable to see a large gathering of infected just on the other side of the vehicle.

The Skells were heading forward to the sound to the helicopter, but had not yet noticed two living persons heading their way. Ivan and Marifi stopped when they saw the way was no longer safe, and Ivan, now gasping for air, leaned backwards onto one of the abandoned vehicles. He did not see the rear window was down, and a zombified woman who had been lying across the back seat. The Skell sprung to life and hurled its body upwards toward the window and latching her teeth into Ivan's forearm.

Ivan yelled while pulled his arm backwards, bringing the creatures head out through the window, allowing Marifi to slice through the woman's think neck with a single swipe.

"FUCK!" Ivan yelled, which alerted every Skell within earshot. One of the original pursuers had now caught up to the couple, biting down into Ivan's shoulder. Ivan bent over forward flipping the skeletal attacker over him onto the ground and he began stomping his foot down on its emaciated stomach, disorienting the creature.

Marifi began swinging her sword widely as arms and teeth came from all directions. Ivan reached for his own blade but realized it had dropped from his belt.

He fell to his knees searching and caught a glimpse of it under the car he had originally leaned on. Marifi now jumped up on to the front hood of that car and continued to swing her blade.

Ivan retrieved his knife, but felt the sharp pain of teeth digging into the arm he was using to stable himself against the side of the car.

"Help me!" he yelled to Marifi who saw a middle-aged man digging his teeth into her man's bicep. She leapt from the car hood and gave the attacker a swift kick in the face, knocking the attacker backwards, but causing her to fall backwards onto the ground. She scrambled to get back up onto the car, but her legs, now extending beyond the hood, were easy targets, and within seconds, they were both being chomped.

She kicked and thrashed to remove the bitters, but not before they had each removed chunks of flesh. Ivan heard her cries and bucked his own attacker off. He stood and charged her two attackers, causing the three of them falling to the ground. Ivan quickly regained his footing and made his way to the car hood. Marifi reached out to grab his arm, but he was so soaked in blood, it took her two attempts to get hold of him. She pulled him up onto the hood and they both climbed onto the roof of the vehicle. The commotion had assembled nearly seventy Skells who were now surrounding the vehicle. Ivan waived his bloody arms in the air to motion BMW to come lower, but Marifi could see from the pilots face that their fate was sealed. Both had been bitten repeatedly.

Ivan and Marifi were know pressed together back to back, as close to the center of the large sedan as they could get, as far away from the dozens of grasping arms reaching for their feet.

BMW could do nothing but watch. He could not get close enough to retrieve them from their location even if he tried. He could see Ivan was yelling and waving his arms for the copter to come down. He looked at Marifi and the two of them made eye contact, just for a second, and then she looked away. He saw her raise her sword, which she had been doing for past few minutes hacking away at the limbs of the infected, but this time she raised it in an unusual position, in the reverse angle of previous thrusts.

Ivan saw the blade before he felt it. It came through with a single quick, steady thrust. In through his back and out through his stomach; the long, bloody blade of Marifi's sword.

'She did it, she killed me,' he thought, until he realized he could still feel her back against his own. He could feel the warmness of their blood pooling together in between.

Marifi had slammed the blade through her own stomach with enough force that it exited her back impaling them both together forever.

And together, they slid slowly down to a sitting position, back to back, on the roof of the car, as their lives drained away.

BMW realized he could do no more and piloted his craft back towards Cape May.

Ivan swallowed hard. He could feel Marifi's heartbeat slowing and her breath becoming more erratic.

"I...I always loved you," he said.

He waited. He did not know, even after all of this, what expect to expect.

Silence.

Marifi thought about all the other men she had seen die over her lifetime. More of them murdered than not. How many had met their end by her own hand. Too many to count, she thought to herself. But ultimately, too few to matter.

Ivan felt Marifi struggle to draw in a deep, final breath.

"I never wanted to kill you," she replied.

Ivan smiled. No one had ever said that to him before.

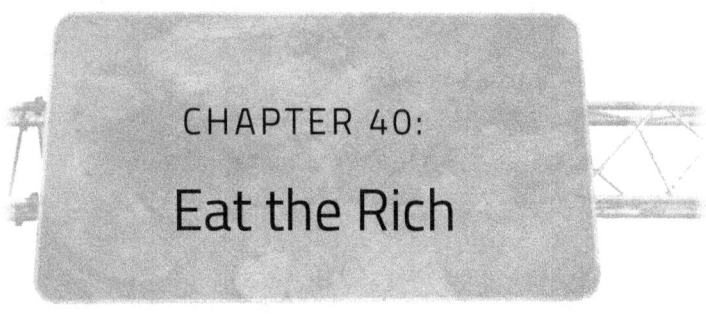

CHAPTER 40:

Eat the Rich

In the President's office, Bankowski came running back into the room. "It's not the laptop, it's the internet. The internet is frozen everywhere. We have no control over it anymore!" Bankowski shrieked.

The laptop screen flickered in unison with the large TV on the office wall. Simultaneously, the new image displayed on the laptop and TV screen was that of Ronan's face. This was the display on all TV, computer and cell phone screens nation-wide. The wall-to-wall coverage which was previously running a news report of the Presidents collapse had been hijacked.

"Citizens." he began. "The President is dead. I have been informed from sources within his inner circle that he has died from a yet unknown ailment, but it seems most likely a heart attack. While I opposed the President as his political advisory, I never wished harm upon him. I too, like our nation, grieve his loss. But now is the time that we must look forward. The last vestige of the former political power structure has now left us. With his death, comes the end of a failed system. Although I am the only announced candidate for your next President, I ask that you still go to the polls tomorrow and vote for me, Ronan, to take this country in a new direction. We have all lost so much. But from this loss, we will find strength and unity. And again G.R.A.SS will grow thick and strong. Thank you."

As the monitors returned to their normal displays, Max and Bankowski quickly returned to the laptop monitor to find Ivan on the bridge CCTV cameras. Bankowski hit keys on the laptop switching from one camera to another. All they saw was blood, Skells and the carnage of shredded victims that would take weeks to identify.

Ivan and Marifi's bodies were no longer on the car roof.

"Where are they?" Max yelled.

"They're dead, don't worry about it Mr. Gold." Bankowski pleaded, trying to save his scalp.

"Don't ever, fucking tell me what I should or should not worry about. You are a worthless piece of shit." Max hissed.

"You are going to take your best men and send them out to that bridge. They will get on their hands and knees and crawl through every piece of flesh, ever pile of guts, every unidentifiable internal organ, and they will find me proof Ivan is dead. Am I clear!?"

Bankowski nearly threw up in his mouth thinking about the task at hand.

Max turned his attention to Daniel Sullivan and Harry Rose. "Mr. Rose, you are the *current* Chief of Staff," Max continued, with emphasis on the word current. "While the President is currently indisposed, you need to take charge of this situation. My first suggestion is that you find this little prick Ronan, and deal with him once and for all. Take Sullivan with you, he is well equipped for this type of thing."

"I'll go with them also." Bankowski volunteered.

"No, you won't." Max sneered. "You will use your facial recognition toy and find Ronan's location. You will provide that location to Mr. Rose and Mr. Sullivan. Then you will go get that fucking Cardinal Remigio and personally escort his ass back to his private jet and get him out of this country and back to the fucking Vatican. Then ensure he is put on the no-fly list. I see him or that giant fucking cross around his neck again, you will be the one crucified. Understand!?"

Stoop shouldered, he picked up his laptop and led Daniel and Rose out of the office.

Max turned too Woodrow and Fiona. "You two, out of this fucking office now! I need to be alone with the President when he comes to. And for Christ sake, Coleman, you better hope he recovers, otherwise it will be you who killed him."

Woodrow began to respond to the old man, but realized it was going to be a futile effort. Fiona put her hand on Woodrow's right shoulder and the two of them exited.

Max, now alone with the President, turned to his former protégé/puppet. He did not care if Patrick Callahan was unconscious; he was going to read this little prick the riot act.

He did not get a chance to share those harsh words though, as Patrick's teeth started ripping out Max's throat.

CHAPTER 41:

Inflicting Policy

Harry Rose had fully returned to his 7322 personae. He did not fit the role of statesman. He would be forced to make compromises. He was not a man of transactional negotiations; he was a man of ideological purity. Compromise breeds contentment, sloth, and gluttony. As he adjusted his PCRC Security Force tactical uniform, he realized that even the brief time out of the uniform had been enough time for he to put on some extra pounds. These were not times to become fat and soft.

Daniel and 7322 entered stealthily into the empty warehouse that was serving as Ronan's campaign headquarters. Ronan had made the mistake of replacing the desktop lamp, thus revealing the origin of his most previous broadcast.

He sat alone, a folding chair in front of small table holding only his laptop and a can of energy drink.

"Go ahead arrest me." Ronan said, not even turning around from his laptop to acknowledge their entrance. "Show the nation how a fascist dictatorship handles its political opposition."

"We're not going to make a martyr out of you." 7322 growled.

"How about we just kill him." Daniel said knowing full well they were not here to harm the little punk in any way. Even a

Sullivan, who punched first and asked questions later, knew that any damage inflicted would only grow the little shit's victimhood.

"Wouldn't help," 7322 replied, "there will always be someone new to take his place. Now we could disarm him, and by that, I mean break his fucking arms so he can't type on his precious little laptop."

Sullivan walked up and stood directly behind Ronan. "Just to be sure, let's break his fingers also."

"Oooh, the cool kids are picking on me in the lunch room." Ronan sneered. He looked up at 7322 who had positioned himself in front of the small table Ronan was using for his computer.

"So, Mr. Rose, I guess you again traded in your name for a number, and traded in your fancy suit for your black pajamas. Your kind is so fucking predictable. You think just because you have that uniform on, you are somebody."

"No son," 7322 replied almost sympathetically. "But I do know that around here, if you don't have this uniform on, you are nobody. And that is what you are. And in a brief period of time, after you have ceased your little internet show, you will be forgotten."

"You can silence me, but the movement has begun. There is no stopping it now." Ronan was in full smug preacher mode. "That is what is great about the internet. It adds permanence to what were once fleeting moments. Even a regime like yours can't control the internet. I will live on forever. Your side has yet to understand that this is now the real world. You are the ones living in the simulation."

7322 was growing weary. "Daniel," he said giving a command that he did not need to elaborate on any further. Daniel Sullivan's large, scared hands grabbed Ronan by the back of the head and neck. He held the man firmly in place while 7322 leaned forward. "Your face has been your greatest asset, hasn't it Ronan, well, time to take that away from you."

Ronan's eyes widened and he struggled, forcing Sullivan to give him a shake and force him to sit still.

7322 reached slowly into his back pocket and withdrew a black object. He brought it around to the side of Ronan's face, just outside his peripheral vision. Ronan heard a click, followed by a beep and then a light was visible. 7322 slowly moved the object into Ronan's field of vision revealing it was a cellphone. 7322 slowly, steadily moved the phone from one side of Ronan's face to the other, capturing a complete 180-degree video of the man's facial features.

7322 examined the just captured imagery on the screen the way most people do when they are ensuring they got a selfie just right. He gave a silent head nod along with a curled bottom lip signifying that he was happy with the photos and video and with a click, he uploaded the data to the cloud.

"I have just added you to the permanence of the web. You are now in our database and should you go anywhere, and I do fucking mean anywhere, we will be able to track you. We can track you indoors if there are smart TV's, security systems, laptops. We can track you outdoors, as soon, ninety percent of the streetlights in this state will have video monitors in them. We will be watching you day and night. We don't need to put you in prison. We don't need to kill you. We will just watch you squirm in your own little reality show. Of course, you won't see it, as we are taking away your screens just like we would a naughty little child. You pick up a phone, it will go dead. You take a tablet into read while you take a dump, it will go dark. You try to surf porn to get your rocks off, the screen will lock up like the worst virus you have seen. You try to get a surrogate to post for you, his digital life will end as well. Your screen privileges have been revoked. Permanently. Hope you like reading books asshole."

As 7322's phone beeped signifying he image had been uploaded, the camera on the laptop in front of Ronan turned on, and within a second, the computer went dark followed by the sound of the hard drive frying.

"Yikes, I hate reading books." Sullivan said as while shaking his head in disgust as he let go of the man, knowing that this bull was now castrated.

"Personally, I like Bret Easton Ellis books." 7322 replied to Sullivan in a casual tone.

Ronan raised his hand to the keyboard and as if he were plunking keys on a piano, pushed down on the keyboard, realizing the laptop was now a doorstop. "You can't monitor all of us. GRASS is more than just me." Ronan said weakly, the possibly of never again being able to access the internet from any device for the rest of his life slowly creeping in.

"If anyone talks to you, we will add them to the database, and soon, once they sit in front of a laptop or check their phone; pfffft. It too will be fried. Soon word will go out that you are patient zero of the web apocalypse. Anyone that comes within ten feet of you will never be able to use an electronic device again. You will be a disease to the disaffected. Alone, discarded, like a used rubber."

"They...they will fight on." Ronan said without confidence.

"Let them. How do you think our side is going to react when they grow tired of your follower's spasms of panic and outrage at everything the President says? Your self-flagellation, hair ripping, near immolation that follows every press conference? Right now, I see a bunch of petulant, ignorant children in the street throwing tantrums. You can hold up your signs, chant your slogans and perform your protest street art. Your efforts are pointless and without any consequence, but basically ignored by our side. A simple annoyance."

"How long do you think this annoyance will be tolerated?"

7322 stepped closer to Ronan, his tone much more ominous. "Our side doesn't do protests." 7322 informed. "What we do is enact policy. You have just seen an example of that. The web is not a right; it is a privilege. A privilege that, just like freedom, can be taken away. And we have just enacted the new policy that if any of your followers get close to you, view your videos, click on your old posts, they will lose that freedom as well. You are patient zero for anonymity. You have lost all internet privileges. No more selfies, no more tweets, no more streaming. Not only can you not post, but you can't view. Word is spreading right at this very moment that anyone who gets close to you, that googles you, that clicks on one of your own links, that views one of your old postings, will lose their privileges for life. Do you realize what I am saying? You are patient zero. You have the disease of no internet access and you are very, VERY, contagious. No one will want to risk being within 100 cyber miles of you."

7322 allowed himself a small smile as he could see the realization creeping across Ronan's face.

"You will never be out of our sight, and you will never be able to go online again. Enjoy your solitude and anonymity."

Sullivan and 7322 walked towards the door from which they entered.

"You many see everything I will do in the future Mr. Rose, but I know everything about your past." Ronan called after them. "I know why you were loyal dog to the old man Gold."

"Good for you." 7322 yelled back without slowing his stride. "You can blog about it. Oh, that's right, you can't"

"Master was what you and the other students had to call him." Ronan said, which made 7322 stop. "He was the head master of the school, but he insisted that the boys only refer to him as Master. In hindsight though HEAD master would have been appropriate per what he was making those little boys do at that private school.

"You were there for a couple years, weren't you? I have heard all the sordid stories of how the Master would manip-ulate the boys in his charge. How he used to be the host of Saturday night skinny-dippings in the pool. How he used to sit on the patio, naked and watch his students frolic. How he would choose certain boys to sit next to him. What an honor that was to be chosen, an envied position, to be placed in that coveted role. Sitting there above all the other boys, naked, next to Master.

"Perhaps you yourself were selected once or twice?

"But you figured out what was going on. You knew something was not right, but your parents would not believe you. On those rare occasions when they would come to the school to visit you, and you confided in them of the strange things that would go on in Master's chambers, would they smack you in the face for saying such horrible things about the well educated, publicly esteemed man who ran that private school. What a horrible child to say such vulgar things about such a great man. Yes, Mr. Rose, I read your files."

Sullivan stood motionless, he just then realized he had never once asked Rose about his past, about anything in his life. Christ, this guy had been a friend and mentor for him since the shit hit the fan and it had not once even occurred to him to know this man. How the hell had he become such a self-centered asshole?

"I believe it was your senior year when you saw the new underclassman arrive." Ronan continued, realizing he had his fish on the hook. "The kid was a several grades below you. Ivan was his name. He was an odd duck. Did not fit in with those upper class rich kids. While he was not there long, he became very involved in your day-to-day life. That is when you met his father Maxwell. A man who would believe you even when your parents didn't, a man who listened to your stories of strange behavior by Master. A man who would bring down that school and ensured Master went to prison. Even today, you remain loyal to that man. Surely you must have figured out by now that Maxwell preyed on you just like Master did? He did not abuse you, but he manipulated and used you. He lured you in with his own flesh and blood, using his own son to reel you in and secure your lifelong fidelity."

Sullivan looked over at the stoic 7322.

"Do you still think about Master still today Harry? About what he did to those boys and how you did nothing to stop him. Do you still have the dreams? You know all too well that there have always been monsters walking the streets. Monsters that stalk, that prey on the innocent. Monsters worse than the Skells because they knew, what they were doing was wrong. But much like zombies, these monsters can also pass their sickness on to others."

7322's breath quickened.

Ronan continued. "You researched online how abused children have a greater chance of becoming abusers as them-selves. Is that why you would not allow yourself to have children of your own Mr. Rose? Because you were afraid that you yourself had become infected from exposure to a monster long ago? A carrier of the worst sickness imaginable."

7322 turned around and faced Ronan.

"Is that why your wife left you? Is that why you are a damaged, lonely man who..."

7322 sprinted towards Ronan and grabbed him by the throat. His forward momentum did not cease, causing Ronan to run backwards on tiptoe, his hands around 7322's wrists trying in vain to free himself.

7322 reached the far wall, slamming Ronan's back against it with such force two windows on the adjacent wall shattered. Ronan was struggling as his throat was being compressed.

Sullivan was still standing in place, taken completely off guard by the sudden change of events. It took him a good thirty seconds to realize that his partner was killing the man.

Sullivan ran over and grabbed 7322's arm to try and free Ronan from the death grip. 7322 pushed him away but Sullivan grabbed the man's arm again with both hands. 7322 let go of Ronan, only to turn his fury on Sullivan. He grabbed the large Irishman by the front of his uniform and threw him to the ground with such force he skidded across the floor.

7322 picked up the coughing Ronan off the floor and again began choking the life out of him.

"You're out of fucking control!" Sullivan yelled as he again came towards his partner, only to get a lightning fast chop to his windpipe, causing him to double over coughing.

Sullivan regained his stature, rubbed his wounded throat, and withdrew his 9mm. "Let the guy go!" he shouted, pointing the gun at his superior and friend.

7322 ignored the command and brought up his knee, catching Ronan in the right leg, shattering his thighbone. Ronan tried to yell out in pain but all that he could muster was a gurgle.

"Harry, please, don't make me do this!" Sullivan shouted.

7322 removed his right hand from the man's throat, grabbed hold of Ronan's left hand that was reaching for his attacker's face, and twisted the hand backwards, snapping the wrist bones.

Sullivan pulled back the hammer. "Please." he pleaded meekly to his friend.

7322 gave the terrorist a final elbow to the nose, and released Ronan to crumple to the floor; a whimpering, choking, mess. His broken nose dripping blood onto his now piss stained pants.

Without saying a word, he turned and again began walking towards the door. Sullivan holstered his firearm, looked over at the crumpled terrorist, and then silently followed behind his boss.

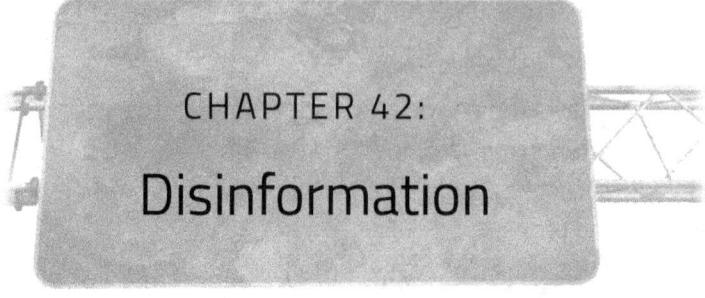

CHAPTER 42:

Disinformation

After devouring Maxwell, Patrick fell into unconscious. He was still out cold when Rose and Sullivan returned.

BMW and Woodrow were summoned to help dispose of Mr. Gold's remains. They rolled him up in a bloodstained rug. Patrick was brought back to his private quarters where Fiona bathed him and removed the chunks of flesh from in between his teeth.

Next, a brainstorming session on how to keep it under wraps that the President had just consumed his former mentor and was now a full blown VINNI.

Harry Rose spoke first. "Look, I know this sounds harsh, but if Patrick had to eat someone, he picked the right guy. No one beyond this group knew that Max was here. The guy is a fugitive, if he is never seen again, everyone will just assume he is in hiding."

Woodrow spoke next. "So, what about Patrick. The public thinks he's dead. Perhaps we should just let them believe that and take him into hiding?" Sullivan chimed in next.

"No way. With him gone, the public will vote for that psychopath Ronan to become the next President. And I tell you what will happen next, everyone in this room be rounded up and arrested. I would not count on any of us surviving the first week of his rule."

"What about the others that saw him lying in this very office dying of a heart attack? That asshole Bankowski and that Vatican guy?" BMW asked.

Rose answered, "I have confirmation that Cardinal Remigio has boarded his private jet back to Rome. He is on his way back to the Vatican. The airport said that the contractor accompanying him decided to board the plane and travel with him as well. So, for now, we are rid of them both. I will ensure Bankowski is put on the no-fly list. Neither he, nor the Cardinal will be returning to the states."

"So, what do we do, let him continue on as the President? You do know what his diet is now don't you." Woodrow remained.

Harry Rose explained the plan. "He does not need to eat all the time. Politicians never eat in public anyway. It is a rule of campaigning, never let the public see you eating." Rose said, his political instincts kicking in.

"We need to get him out into the public immediately, like tomorrow. We need him giving speeches and shaking hands. The media has video of him collapsing, for all they know, he's dead. We need to calm the country by showing them that he is still alive and in charge. Going forward we keep his public appearances limited. We only do interviews with selected, friendly media, who will stick to pre-approved questions. We all know he is sick, but if anyone asks, deny, deny, deny."

"Well what happens if he starts going...well...you know, he gets hungry again?" BMW asked.

Sullivan spoke up. "There is a special van in the Presidential motorcade. It is one of those oversized black Mercedes vans, the kind with the high roof. Normally, we store medical equipment up in the roof compartment, because it's specially air conditioned to keep those supplies cool."

"Yeah, so how is that going to help us?" Woodrow asked.

"We keep the van stocked." Sullivan replied. "If we notice him out in public and he is getting wobbly, we rush him into that van and we give him what he needs. By the time the van arrives at the next stop, we have him fed, cleaned up, and good as new again. Anyone asks why he appears the way he does, we tell them he has the flu."

"You are not saying..." Woodrow began.

"Look, think of him as a diabetic. When he is out in public, we just need to ensure he has his insulin nearby. If he starts to go a bit wobbly, Sullivan and BMW will each grab an arm to keep him steady, we hustle him into the van and drive off and give him what he needs." Rose said.

"You mean people. Instead of insulin we will be feeding him body parts, human body parts, in that van?" Woodrow asked.

"Yes, human body parts. We are not going to be letting him loose to go out and hunt people, we will have a supply of body parts for him." Sullivan explained.

"And no one will notice we keep hustling the President into the mystery mobile?" Woodrow asked.

"Let me make sure I am understanding this." BMW chimed in.

"We will be driving him to each of his campaign stops in a van stocked with human flesh and body parts that we need to feed to him every couple of hours?"

"Yes." Rose replied. "The polls open in twenty-four hours. As insane as it sounds, it is the only thing we can do right to keep this country from tearing itself apart. We have a zombie as President."

"Where exactly are we supposed to get a steady supply of coolers, full of fresh body parts?" Woodrow asked.

Sullivan pulled out his cell phone and hit the speed dial. "I am going to call Ragu."

CHAPTER 43:
The Government They Deserve

Forty-eight hours later, on a closed commercial runway at the Newark Airport, next to the multicolored, newly named, PCRC Sports Arena, Patrick gave the most rousing speech of his Presidency. He thanked the voters for their support and asked them to vote for him in the following special election. He touted success and brought to their attention that there was not an infected person to be seen. He talked about normalcy and restored security. He talked about the thousands of new jobs his administration would be creating with the national and global expansion of PCRC and the Contractors. He talked about the prosperity coming from this new workforce. Skilled jobs for scientists, architects, bio technicians and urban planners. High wage blue collar jobs for truck drivers and infected collection specialists. Specialty jobs in personal protection, physical and cyber security.

He then addressed the rest of the world.

The Malthusian catastrophe had come true, but to fear not, the United States had the solution.

He notified all world leaders, friend and foe, that new ambassadors from his administration would be dispatched to all corners of the globe to discuss this new US export.

America was once again the producer of goods that the world would die for.

President Patrick Callahan felt the waves of admiration from the crowd race towards him. He was the President of a new age. The public could not put their finger on it, but they just knew he was unprecedented. The first of his kind to hold the office.

He looked over across the stage to see his newly chosen Vice President Harry Rose. Standing next to Harry was his new Chief of Staff Daniel Sullivan, and just past him, stood James Sullivan, along with BMW, both in their crisp new contractor uniforms. The two men stood next to a tall black presidential van that had replaced the usual Presidential limo. Inside that van sat Science Czar Woodrow Wilson and Fiona Sullivan, ready to assist the President.

The day before President Sullivan had become unsteady and almost collapsed. The episode was caught on a cellphone camera and quickly went viral. "It was just a combination of the flu and allergies," his press secretary informed the public. A quick drive in the van, a private bite to eat, followed by a change of clothes and a generous number of wet-wipes, and the President was out in public again looking fresh and invigorated. Ready to meet the next challenge. But there were no shaking of hands and kissing of babies at this airport event. He could not get too close to the public and would always be surrounded by his Contractors. After all, there were still dangers out there.

Why, just a day earlier, and just across the street from the airport, the Presidents advance security detail had arrested two men whom they found bound, gagged and naked in the meadowlands swamp. They were ranting about being robbed of their clothes and private jet. They were taken to the hospital for observation.

In the sky above Rome, two other men were waking from a long flight. One of the men adjusted his ill-fitting vestments as he gazed out the window hoping for a glimpse of the Vatican. The place where his journey had begun so long ago. A lifetime ago it seemed. Pope Judas of Jersey would finally take back his rightful place in the world.

ABOUT THE AUTHOR

Neil A. Cohen has spent the past twenty years working with federal, state, and local government agencies supporting emergency management and counter terrorism. He has worked military agencies in the USA, as well as South America, Asia, Europe, and the Middle East. He has found that one of the favorite topics of military and responder agencies worldwide is the zombie apocalypse and how they would manage the crisis when it inevitably occurs. The knowledge, concepts, and ideas of apocalypse management that he has gathered from around the globe have been distilled down into his books *Exit Zero*, *Nuke Jersey*, and *Zombie Democracy*. Neil has been happily married for over twenty years to his wife Vicki, the real Marifi, and has two daughters Sasha and Hannah.

PERMUTED
PRESS
needs **you** to help

SPREAD (THE)
INFECTION

FOLLOW US!

f | Facebook.com/PermutedPress
🐦 | Twitter.com/PermutedPress

REVIEW US!

Wherever you buy our book, they can be
reviewed! We want to know what you like!

GET INFECTED!

Sign up for our mailing list at
PermutedPress.com

PERMUTED
PRESS

KING ARTHUR AND THE KNIGHTS OF THE ROUND TABLE HAVE BEEN REBORN TO SAVE THE WORLD FROM THE CLUTCHES OF MORGANA WHILE SHE PROPELS OUR MODERN WORLD INTO THE MIDDLE AGES.

EAN 9781618685018 $15.99   **EAN** 9781682611562 $15.99

Morgana's first attack came in a red fog that wiped out all modern technology. The entire planet was pushed back into the middle ages. The world descended into chaos.

But hope is not yet lost— King Arthur, Merlin, and the Knights of the Round Table have been reborn.

THE ULTIMATE PREPPER'S ADVENTURE.
THE JOURNEY BEGINS HERE!

EAN 9781682611654 $9.99   **EAN** 9781618687371 $9.99   **EAN** 9781618687395 $9.99

The long-predicted Coronal Mass Ejection has finally hit the Earth, virtually destroying civilization. Nathan Owens has been prepping for a disaster like this for years, but now he's a thousand miles away from his family and his refuge. He'll have to employ all his hard-won survivalist skills to save his current community, before he begins his long journey through doomsday to get back home.

PERMUTED
PRESS

THE MORNINGSTAR STRAIN HAS BEEN LET LOOSE—IS THERE ANY WAY TO STOP IT?

An industrial accident unleashes some of the Morningstar Strain. The

EAN 9781618686497 $16.00

doctor who discovered the strain and her assistant will have to fight their way through Sprinters and Shamblers to save themselves, the vaccine, and the base. Then they discover that it wasn't an accident at all—somebody inside the facility did it on purpose. The war with the RSA and the infected is far from over.

This is the fourth book in Z.A. Recht's The Morningstar Strain series, written by Brad Munson.

PERMUTED
PRESS

GATHERED TOGETHER AT LAST, THREE TALES OF FANTASY CENTERING AROUND THE MYSTERIOUS CITY OF SHADOWS...ALSO KNOWN AS CHICAGO.

EAN 9781682612286 $9.99   **EAN** 9781618684639 $5.99   **EAN** 9781618684899 $5.99

From *The New York Times* and *USA Today* bestselling author Richard A. Knaak comes three tales from Chicago, the City of Shadows. Enter the world of the Grey—the creatures that live at the edge of our imagination and seek to be real. Follow the quest of a wizard seeking escape from the centuries-long haunting of a gargoyle. Behold the coming of the end of the world as the Dutchman arrives.

Enter the City of Shadows.

PERMUTED
PRESS

WE CAN'T GUARANTEE
THIS GUIDE WILL SAVE
YOUR LIFE. BUT WE CAN
GUARANTEE IT WILL
KEEP YOU SMILING
WHILE THE LIVING
DEAD ARE CHOWING
DOWN ON YOU.

EAN 9781618686695 $9.99

This is the only tool you need to survive the zombie apocalypse.

OK, that's not really true. But when the SHTF, you're going to want a survival guide that's not just geared toward day-to-day survival. You'll need one that addresses the essential skills for true nourishment of the human spirit. Living through the end of the world isn't worth a damn unless you can enjoy yourself in any way you want. (Except, of course, for anything having to do with abuse. We could never condone such things. At least the publisher's lawyers say we can't.)

PERMUTED
PRESS